PRAISE FOR *MAY WE SHED THESE HUMAN BODIES*

"Sparks's debut story collection swirls with a Tim Burton-like whimsy....modern fables in which epiphanies replace moral lessons and tales unfold with Grimm-like wickedness."

—*Publishers Weekly*

"I always love a book that makes me fear for the writer's sanity. I'm over here praying for Amber Sparks."

—Ben Loory, author of *Stories for Nighttime and Some for the Day*

"There was Aesop, Thomas Bulfinch, Edith Hamilton, Angela Carter—and now there is Amber Sparks with a new take on the fable. *May We Shed These Human Bodies* is a clever, scary, and charming debut collection full of great imagination."

—Michael Kimball, author of *Big Ray* and *Dear Everybody*

"In *May We Shed These Human Bodies*, Amber Sparks proves herself not only a fine writer but also a high scientist of imaginative bliss: This is a collection of marvelous inventions, each one a wonder-machine propelled by fairy tale and dream and humor and hope, ready to carry us off into new adventure."

—Matt Bell, author of *Cataclysm Baby*

"THIS BOOK IS AMAZING. MAKES *FIFTY SHADES OF GREY* LOOK LIKE *TWILIGHT* FAN FICTION."

—Amelia Gray, author of *Threats* and *Museum of the Weird*

MAY WE SHED THESE HUMAN BODIES

Stories

AMBER SPARKS

A CURBSIDE SPLENDOR BOOK

CHICAGO INDEPENDENT PUBLISHING

CURBSIDE SPLENDOR PUBLISHING

Published by Curbside Splendor Publishing, Inc., Chicago, Illinois in 2012.

First Edition
Copyright © 2012 by Amber Sparks
Library of Congress Control Number: 2012948224

ISBN 978-0-9834228-7-7

Edited by Lauryn Allison Lewis
Designed by Alban Fischer

Manufactured in the United States of America.

www.curbsidesplendor.com

contents

For Loki, who for ten years was my furry armrest, my (mostly) rapt audience, and my constant companion as I wrote these stories. He is present in all of these pages.

death and the people

When Death came and started it all, the people on Earth had already drawn close together to wait for spring. The trees were bare, but expectant, and the pale yellow light was starting to filter though the shades slantwise, a little later every day. The people were feeling luxurious. They were knees between elbows, chins tilted upward like cats in the sun. The new warmth danced on their spines and fingers and made them feel all tingly, and they were almost silent with the happiness of it all.

Everything was perfect, thought the people. Everything was good.

Then Death walked in and totally ruined the mood. He stood tall and elegant and kind of preppy in a crisp white button-down and chinos. He cleared his throat, and the people waited. Finally, he pointed at one of the people and said, Come with me.

There was an awkward silence. The people sat still, unmoving. No, really, said Death, after a minute or so. I haven't got all day. Let's go.

The people made a sudden and impulsive decision. No, they said, holding tighter to one another's knees and elbows. We belong together. You can't take one of us.

Death was annoyed. This had never happened before. He looked pointedly at his watch, hoping to telegraph his annoyance. He was, frankly, freezing cold. It was spring in the Afterwards already, and Death was wearing loafers without socks.

The people just sat there and stared at him. There sure were a lot of them today. If he goes, they said, then we all go. We're totally serious about this.

I can't take you all, said Death. Maybe a few dozen of you. But hurry up and decide on who. We've got to get going.

No, said the people. None of us want to be left here alone.

The people were really starting to piss Death off. He looked at his watch again and wondered what would happen if he brought them all back. Was there enough room in the Afterwards? Would he get in trouble with the Ones in Charge? The door was still open, and he wondered if he should just walk out, pretend this never happened, and come back later when the people were in a better mood. The people could be such children sometimes.

This is the way things are, said Death. You can't change the way things are. But the people were defiant and stared back stone-eyed, and he knew it would be useless to keep arguing with them. The people always wanted to change the way things were.

So Death gave in. Fine, he said. Fine. You all have to come with me, then. And you can't come back, understand? You can't ever come back. Remember I told you that.

Sure, said the people, not really listening. They smiled and followed Death out the door, miles and miles of them flying behind in a trailing clump like migratory birds. If there had been any people left on Earth, they would have marveled at the vast human inkblot spreading across the sky.

Free of the people, the Earth shook itself off like a wet dog. The people had been a heavy weight. It got to work quickly, destroying all the people's stuff; drowning it, painting it with mold, cracking it in half and blowing it up. The people watched from their crowded dwellings in the Afterwards, suddenly sorry about their chairs and cars and books. We were one, said the people, and none of us would leave without the other—but I mean, come on! That was an autographed, first-edition copy of *The Grapes of Wrath*! There were no books in the Afterwards, which the people thought was some serious bullshit.

In fact, there wasn't much of anything in the Afterwards. The people were supposed to try and ease out of being human now, but that seemed like kind of a drag. The people had liked being human. They took to watching the Earth from the basement window of the Afterwards, watching progress play out like a faraway filmstrip. It was a long, bitter movie without them, but they couldn't stop watching. They wanted to see how it would end.

The people could see that Earth wasn't able get rid of everything at first. Some of the weapons the people left behind were dangerous, and Earth couldn't figure out what to do with them. It tried to bury them, but they leaked and leaked, contaminating the water and the soil. Animals ate the bad fruits that grew in the soil and got all messed up; lots of them died, intestines turned inside out and soaked in battery acid and radium.

After a while, though, it seemed like everything started to grow and adapt, including the animals and the plants. Highways cracked and at first looked naked without their blanket of traffic, but soon they were modestly draped in green as moss, and weeds and flowers pushed up through the gaps in the concrete. The skyscrapers buckled and bent, while the trees shoved branches through the glass panes. After a few centuries, everything the people had made was buried or gone. Everything except the structures of stone that were put up long before the memories of the people had even begun.

The people were not happy about all of this. They went to Death and demanded to know why Earth had destroyed all the awesome stuff they made when they were alive. That stuff took a long time to build, said the people. We worked really hard on it, you know?

Death said, why would the Earth need people-things without

people around? You should quit bothering me, anyway—I have a date tonight and I have to get ready.

The people got all pouty and refused to go. They stood in Death's doorway and watched him roll up his shirtsleeves just so, and create a sharp part in his hair with his tortoiseshell comb. Even though they were mad at Death, the people had to admit he was awfully stylish. Death looked kind of like a J. Crew model.

Well, said Death, are you going to get out of my way?

No, said the people. We're bored. There's nothing to do here. We miss Earth.

And whose fault is that, said Death. You were the ones that insisted on coming. You were the ones who said you couldn't be left there. Death put his loafers on and tried to push past the people, but they blocked his path, their elbows locked together. They were crying a little.

We didn't know, they said. You never told us what it was like to be dead. We didn't know how lame it would be.

Keep each other company, said Death, slipping out the back door instead.

The people walked sadly, dejected, down the streets of the Afterwards. They tired of each other's company and tried to find quiet places alone, but it was too crowded. When the people came all at once, they'd filled up all of the nooks and crannies of the whole Afterwards. If the people wanted privacy they had to close their eyes and pretend.

They started to resent Death a whole lot. He just kept coming around and ruining stuff, breaking up couples and shutting the basement window so they couldn't see the Earth anymore. Come on, guys, said Death. Forget about being alive.

So the people started calling Death 'The Hall Monitor'. Behind his back, of course. And they only became more stubborn, more determined to remember. They thought about winter, and sports, and their cats and dogs, their guinea pigs. They dreamed of central heating, and flat-screen TVs, and jump ropes and credit cards and studying. They remembered being drunk, and swimming in chlorinated pools, and falling asleep to music at night, and having babies, and being in love, and picking up pennies on the sidewalk, and sometimes believing in anything and sometimes in nothing at all. They missed the long drum roll of history, and were sorry to have cut it off so abruptly. And the people became more and more restless.

Death watched the people and worried they were going to cause problems. They had no intention of adapting to the Afterwards; that much was clear. He worried that maybe they would start rioting or something. The people are bored, thought Death. They need something to occupy their time.

So Death built the people a giant movie megaplex, the largest in the universe, where they could watch any movie ever made. And the people were thrilled. They forgot their basement window and spent all their time at the movies, dropping popcorn on the floor through buttery fingers and drinking fountain sodas with plastic straws. They formed film discussion groups, arguing the merits of German Expressionism versus Neo-Realism, and Police Academy sequels versus stoner comedies. They watched fast car chases and slow love scenes with equal ardor, and their skin turned translucent and pale as milk from so many days spent in the dark. Death sighed in relief and stopped worrying.

But then one morning, when Death was brushing his teeth, he looked in the mirror and saw the people standing there all disgruntled-looking. Death spat into the sink and said, Oh, great. What now?

We long for Earth, said the people. It's time we went back.

Jesus, said Death. What is the deal with you people? Are you tired of your movie theater already? Did you run out of movies?

No, said the people. We love the movie theater. In fact, we have a long list of movies we still want to see.

So what's the problem? Death asked. He was glad he had a bathrobe on. The people had to stop dropping in like this. It was like the people didn't understand that Death needed some privacy.

The people fidgeted and shuffled their feet, and Death was gratified to see that they at least seemed a little embarrassed. We love the movies, they said, but they all remind us of Earth. And now we're more homesick than ever.

Death felt sorry for the people, in spite of their popping up uninvited all the time. They couldn't help that they always had bad timing, that they always did the wrong thing. That was what the people were like. You can't go back, he said gently. I told you that before. Is there something else that you would like? Something that would make you happier here?

Sandwiches, said the people. And lipstick. And cell phones. And swimming pools, and losing weight, and relaxing on beach towels, and telling white lies, and growing things. We want snow and museums and political rallies and sex and cigarettes and tree trunks and ripe apples and hunting rifles and pizza and shopping malls and nightmares and bonfires. The people stood with their arms crossed, waiting.

Death had no idea what to do. He figured he'd better ask the Ones in Charge, so he rinsed off his toothbrush, placed it neatly in the toothbrush holder, and walked to the bedroom to change out of his bathrobe. The people followed, arms still crossed mulishly. Look, said Death, lifting a grey cashmere sweater out of his top drawer. Can you please get out of here? I need to get dressed.

How come we don't get to wear cashmere? Or brush our teeth, or wear loafers without socks? the people asked.

Because you're dead, said Death.

Being dead is getting old, said the people.

Let me talk to the Ones in Charge and see what I can do, said

Death. Now leave me alone so I can get dressed in privacy. Please.

We'll go, said the people. But we'll be back. We're not giving up.

Death was starting to understand why he felt sympathy for the people, why he was even beginning to grow fond of them. They were so brave and stubborn in the face of things that couldn't be changed. Even dead, they clung to their sense of what it meant to be living, and they seemed utterly unable to give it up. Over the eons, Death had watched countless beings shed life like a skin, wriggling free and wrapping themselves in the elemental instead. Most beings seemed to delight in losing the weight of the world. But the people held hard to weight, to the heaviest things like furniture and loss and other people. They seemed determined to be solid, to be planted—to be unavoidable roadblocks in the flow of the Afterwards. They were strange beings, the people. There was nothing else like them.

Death flew up to the attic of the Afterwards where the Ones in Charge hung out. They were playing *Mario Kart Wii*, and it took Death what seemed like a year and a half to get their attention. Well, said the Ones. You wanted to see us about something?

Uh, he said, yes. The people have started to revolt. They want to go back to Earth. I told them they can't, but it doesn't seem to matter.

Hmm, said the Ones. Death was pretty sure they weren't even listening. The Ones in Charge were so annoying when they were playing video games. When they first got a copy of *Gears of War*, they refused to see anyone except Death for two whole weeks. Plus Death had to keep bringing them Doritos and Hot Pockets.

Guys, he said. Guys, come on—the people are totally harassing me. They just keep showing up at my house. You have to do something.

The Ones didn't even look away from the TV when they spoke to Death. You think we hadn't noticed? That we were just totally ignorant up here? I mean, seriously. We are the Ones in Charge. We know everything.

Well, then, asked Death, what should I do? With the people, I mean?

Take them back to Earth, said the Ones in Charge. We're bored, too. We used to get our kicks watching the people. Now we have nothing to do.

For real? Death asked. Send them back to Earth? I can do that?

Yes, and do it quickly, said the Ones in Charge. Aren't you bored, too, Death?

Well, yeah, but—I mean, if I let them go back, I'm just going to look like a giant pussy, said Death.

Nah, I wouldn't worry about that. You're already a giant pussy anyway, said the Ones in Charge, and high-fived each other.

Hey, said Death. But then he realized he pretty much was.

Go to the people, said the Ones in Charge. Take them back now, but don't let them remember. Give them a fresh start. Earth will help you.

And so Death assembled all the people in the public square and delivered the good news. It was something he was unused to doing, so he stammered a little, but when he told the people they would get to go back they put him on their shoulders and cheered. They promised never to call him 'The Hall Monitor' ever again, and to be super-ultra respectful of Death in the future. They even poured fountain soda all over him, since they didn't have any Gatorade in the Afterwards. Death had to admit he was a little touched by the gesture, even if he was all sticky now.

At last it was time for the people to return to Earth. So Death showered and put on his best black suit, and flew to Earth with the people in tow. The people were soft and pale and slow by now, so it took a long time to get everybody back. Then Death erased the people's memories, and took away their language, and set them on the plains and hills, and in the forests and jungles and deserts, naked and full of ideas and newness.

Earth was secretly pleased to see the people again. It had been caring for the animals, and that was kind of interesting, for a while. All the new plants, too. Thing was, though, the animals and plants never really surprised you like the people could. Some of the people's surprises had been horrible, to be sure. And Earth had seriously resented the people for it. But Earth thought maybe this time it could improve the people, push them in the right direction every now and then. Maybe the people just needed a firm hand.

Fruits and vegetables grew like crazy to make the people strong. The water ran clear and cold, skimmed over silver rocks, and poured itself into the people's hands to refresh them. The animals rubbed against the people's legs, and the sky made sunshine and plump white clouds to sit under. And the people marveled at their existence and invented language, and the first thing they spoke of was how they came to be.

to make us whole

Robert and I were supposed to pay for the new bathtub somehow, since we were the ones who broke the old one. Helen told on us, so we decided to hate her with a fierce and burning hatred for all time, but *then* Mother started crying and told us we'd have to be nice to our brothers and sisters now because they were the only friends we'd ever have. And then Mother forgot all about us paying for the bathtub, so we decided we didn't have to hate Helen after all. We decided to join in solidarity with her to fight Mother's new strangeness instead.

We'd all been avoiding Mother. Since Father died she'd been pacing the halls at night, weeping like anything, making these ghastly drawings on our walls of things that maybe were clouds, but if you looked closer the maybe-clouds were raining blood. Mother had always sketched, of course, but now that we were poor she couldn't afford drawing paper, and her pencils were down to nubs. We weren't sure what she would do when they were gone. Mother had tried to explain to us, after we first found the drawings, that she wasn't feeling very well just now. That wasn't surprising. Father had shot himself in the head after being discovered in Disgrace. We didn't know what kind of Disgrace, but apparently it was the catching kind because we were all in it, too. We didn't care what other people thought, but Mother took it hard. She came from a very old family and she was very proud. Helen said it was the Disgrace that was making Mother crazy.

It was Helen who also discovered what the new bathtub could do. It started as an accident. Mother had given her Father's gold wedding ring, since Helen was the only one of us who really knew him; she was old enough to remember him before he was in the service. Helen was still awfully attached to Father, and had strung his ring on a gold chain that she wore around her neck every day since they buried him. The day the bathtub came was also the day the clasp broke and the ring slipped off, right into the tub as Helen was filling it, and before she could fish it out, golden tendrils shot up through the suds, forking and twisting round one another in complex spirals and braids. Scarlet rubies the size of cherries burst from the gold and hung heavy and fat on the branches. Helen ran screaming for Mother, who took one look and sort of crumpled like paper onto the tile. Robert finally had the sense to pull the plug, and once the water was drained, the golden tree stopped growing.

After the tree incident Mother kept a close eye on us, sitting next to the tub with a book while she drew the bath. She'd hidden the golden tree away in the upstairs linen closet. She didn't want a repeat of the incident, but we were children, after all. We were determined to experiment further. So one afternoon, Helen tiptoed into the bathroom and casually laid a small piece of lace from her doll's apron flat on the floor of the tub. It was bleached white, so thin you could see right through to the cream colored ceramic underneath. Helen and Robert and I all peeked around the corner when Mother started the bath for James, the baby.

Nothing happened.

We all sighed in disappointment, especially Helen, who really wanted a lace dress. She felt the bathtub owed her after Father's ring, and besides, we'd lost all of our money in the Disgrace and our clothes were terribly out of fashion. Well, at least according to Helen, who cared about that sort of thing. It's just too bad, she said, and kicked at the floor. Stupid bathtub.

No, no, wait, said Robert. Look. Look there! Sure enough, we could just about see something—yes, the tip of a long lace sleeve poking out of the water like a snake's head and hovering above the surface. It was followed by another sleeve. Then the two sleeves reached into the water like arms and pulled out their other half, a white lace bodice with a long, trailing skirt. The dress hung in midair for a moment as we all watched, frozen in fascination, then wrung itself out all over the floor and draped itself over the towel rack.

Mine, it's mine, shrieked Helen, and she dashed into the bathroom and grabbed for the wet lace. Our very grim, very white-faced Mother dragged her into the master bedroom, and we winced and tried not to listen to the spanking or the sobbing. Helen and I shared a room, and she kept me up all night complaining of the injustice. It's not fair, she kept saying, over and over again until the darkness faded into grey. In the morning Mother announced that as soon as she could arrange it, the bathtub was going back. We all groaned, but Mother's tight mouth and clenched hands signaled that was the end of it. No more incidents. No more bathtub.

Before it went back, though, Robert wanted to shock us. He knew he'd get in bad trouble, so he wanted to go as explosive as possible to justify the bad. That was Robert all over. He crept in while I was bathing, and stood still and silent behind Mother, who was washing my hair and didn't hear him come in. He pushed a pin into the pad of his index finger, winking at me over Mother's shoulder. Robert slowly extended his finger above Mother's head out over the tub, and I saw a single drop of blood hang there for just a second before it splashed into the water. Mother's head whipped around. No, no, I yelled, kicking and flailing and trying to get away from the thing that was already streaming up out of the wet. It was hard to tell just what it was at first, but as the blood droplets joined up and the veins grew around the dark red river, as the joints formed and bits of cartilage clicked together like rocks, then tissue draped over muscle draped over bone—it became clear that the thing was an arm. An arm still waiting to be made whole. It wiggled its fingers at me, and I screamed and scrambled, naked and wet, up and over the side of the tub, landing hard on my tailbone on the cold tile. And before anyone could move, that horrible arm grabbed Robert's collar and pulled hard—pulled him under so fast we barely saw him go. We all reached in, feeling for anything that could have been our brother, but he had disappeared. He and the arm and everything else.

What happens when a brother goes in? asked Helen. None of us could guess. I tried fishing around for the plug. Mother sat down on the toilet and looked at the bathtub, looking and looking and not saying a word. It was whisper quiet, horror quiet, until suddenly a throbbing, thrumming sound started coming from the bathtub. The tub started shaking so hard all four of its clawed feet came loose. Then it fell over with a loud thud, sending soapy water sliding over the floor and seven life-sized dolls—no, people—sliding out with it.

We watched the bathtub people unfold themselves and they watched us right back, dripping and smiling. Robert was one of them. Mother's throat made a tea kettle sound when she saw him. He just stood there still and strange, his eyes black instead of green, like he didn't know Mother or any of us at all. And next to him there was a black-eyed Helen, a black-eyed, fat-cheeked James, a black-eyed me, a black-eyed Mother, and a black-eyed Father with a gaping hole in his head. But he was smiling, too. They were all lined up, limbs slightly askew, like marionettes, and they smiled and smiled and smiled at us.

Hello, we said to ourselves.

Hello, said ourselves to us.

the dictator is
drinking alone

The dictator is drinking alone, watching Shane and weeping into a glass of whiskey.

Well, not entirely alone. His Special Guard is there, of course, dressed in grey and scarlet uniforms with matching marching band hats. But the Guard doesn't count as company. They're an extension of him, an extra set of senses always at the ready.

The dictator is fiftyish, fattish, short. He sits in a giant wingback chair with oaken arms carved to look like antlers and cattle hide stretched over the frame. The dictator is obsessed with the American West, and he spends afternoons watching his collection of Western DVDs on his 72 inch flatscreen TV.

When the Americans come to meet with him, he likes to shame them by drinking straight whiskey while they politely ask for a brandy and soda. The dictator understands that American men no longer have any balls, like when they used to herd cattle and hang men from trees. Now they drink like little girls, with tiny sips, nervousness written all over their milky faces.

The dictator despises the Americans. They are nothing like cowboys. They are big, yes, but stupid and loud and vain. They no longer wear hats, and their eyes are watery, evasive. They are shifty. They talk too much. And American women—he hates the American women most of all. They are taller than him, with big feet and big hands. He's not sure that they don't have big penises too, hidden beneath those voluminous slacks.

He shakes his head in disgust at the thought, and watches Shane climb up onto his horse. The dictator is the Number One National Champion of Riding, although he has never actually been on a horse. He is terrified of live animals. He is also the Number One National Champion of Fishing, Wrestling, Golf, Racquetball, Archery, Volleyball, Shooting, and General Fitness Excellence.

The dictator's son walks into the room. General Comrade Father, he says, what the shit are you crying for?

I'm not crying, you ungrateful prick, says the dictator, pausing the DVD. It's the whiskey. It burns my throat and makes my eyes water.

His son flashes a sly, stupid grin. You should be more careful of your health, General Comrade Father. You drink too much. He's the youngest son, the idiot, and the one that will succeed the dictator if the military has its way. Oh, and General Comrade Father, he asks now, can I have some money?

The dictator sighs loudly, pointedly. He is long-suffering. I just gave you money, he says. What the hell do you need more for? Prostitutes? Vodka? Coffee? Guns? What?

Prostitutes, says the son brightly, as if it were a multiple-choice question. The dictator nods at the Guardsman to his right. Get him some cash, he says. And get him out of my sight before I blow his testicles off with my new Tokarev.

The dictator collects Russian weapons, particularly World War II-era pistols. He practices with them regularly from his balcony. When someone gets shot, if they're not mortally wounded, they're supposed to fall down on their knees and thank the heavens that the General Great Leader is such an excellent marksman. If they're mortally wounded they're supposed to just lie there quietly and die.

Once his son has gone to his prostitutes, the dictator hits the pause button to resume the movie. Shane is telling Joey to grow up strong, to take care of his parents. The dictator picks up his glass and tilts it sideways, watches the liquid slosh around and coat the sides like amber.

The truth is, the dictator is bored and sad. The truth is, the dictator is crying, and not because the whiskey burns. He's crying because he knows Joey will never see Shane again, will grow up without a hero, will grow up weak and restless and wanting. He's weeping because Shane has gone into the mountains for good.

the chemistry of objects

Exhibit 5WW: Metal Canister. Discovered at Majdanek, 1944.

The casual observer may, at first glance, mistake the canister behind the glass for a dented coffee can. The label is almost entirely gone, the faded gold paper clinging in shreds to the flaking, rusted metal. But if the visitor looks closely at the largest shred they may make out a group of small black letters, gone indigo with age and sun. Giftgas! the letters shout. How funny it sounds, like a child's party favor. How exciting! A handful of bright plastic packets. Laughing gas tied off with curled satin ribbons.

But the letters do not shout in English, and the contents of the canister were never meant to be merry. The word is German. The English translation: poison gas. This can is not a coffee can, and it has never contained beans or laughing gas or party favors; it has instead poured pellets of gas into sealed chambers through special vents, smothering those inside. Polish Jews who'd never seen the sea drowned in their own blood.

Exhibit 144G: Grecian urn engraved with images of the Siege of Kirrha, circa 590 B.C.

The history of chemistry starts with a greed for gold. But soon after greed comes process, then order, then method, and the method improves over time. Paracelsus, Boyle, Lavoisier, Dalton—they demand rigor and develop theory. And as they mix and measure and observe reactions—the making and breaking of chemical bonds—it is not alchemy, not magic and spells and incantations, but chemistry. Hard, precise work, in the service of something more.

There is also a parallel history, its stain spreading in the shadow of chemistry. It begins in earnest with alchemy, but really, has always bedded down with war. Chinese writings from 1000 B.C. describe a "soul-hunting fog" filled with arsenic. In the West, there is the poisoning of wells—first by the Greeks, then by the Germanic tribes at war with the Romans. To this last, the Romans respond nobly, armis bella non venenis geri. War is fought with weapons, not with poisons. Which would be admirable prose save for the Romans' own tainting of enemy wells in Anatolia.

Chemical warfare is chemistry's hideous offspring, locked away in the attic until its grotesqueries are required. Leonardo DaVinci proposes making a powder of chalk, sulfide of arsenic, and verdigris. He recommends launching this powder at enemy ships with projectiles, in order to asphyxiate those on board.

In 1854, a British chemist suggests the use of chlorine-filled shells to end the siege of Sevastopol. He is roundly rebuked by the British Ordnance Department for bad form, but simply shrugs. No doubt in time, he says, chemistry will be used to lessen the suffering of combatants. No doubt in time.

Like Frankenstein, we become dangerous makers. Our hearts lean toward what burns in nature, and whether for pleasure or profit, through accident or malice, we create what kills best. And try as we might, we cannot seem to climb out of this paradox. We are monkeys with test tubes, apes at the evolutionary table. The big brains.

Exhibit 23W: 9 mm Luger pistol, manufactured in
Germany, 1911.

It is 1915, and a couple is arguing. He is quick, canny, but also by
turns saturnine; he can sink faulty logic with a single dry shot. He
is a well-known wit, well-respected in the scientific community: a
brilliant, brainy chemist.

But then again, so is she. And she is turning his arguments inside
out, spreading their guts on the dining room table and picking them
carefully apart. He says he has discovered a way to end the war. She
raises an eyebrow. He says he wants peace, only peace—but he is
also a good Prussian nationalist, and he loves his country. And he
loves his country winning.

Ach, Fritz, she says. It goes against everything, everything we do.
She is a pacifist, a romantic idealist; when emotional she becomes
raw energy bubbling over. It's immoral, she says. It's inhuman. She
says everything she can think of, everything to win the argument.

But she has already lost. His resolve is hardened toward the
weapons of war. And so in the spring of 1915, he will put his idea
into practice and release chlorine gas from pressurized cylinders
at Ypres, allowing the wind to carry it over the enemy's trenches.
French and Algerian boys will watch the creeping gas cloud, green
and sulfurous, more surprised than anything as they begin to choke
on their own breath.

He will be pleased with his success.

That night, her neurons will refuse to stop firing, refuse to
stop etching a Mobius strip of dying men across the inside of her
eyelids. She will not find relief or release from all that blood until she
remembers his army pistol: a blunt instrument, and a simple answer
to the series of complex processes that add up to her.

Standing alone in the garden, she will use classical mechanics
to combat chemistry, and an object in motion tends to stay in

motion—until it meets bone and flesh and a critical mass of muscle. Or to put it another way: a bullet will travel along a certain path at a certain velocity, propelled by a striking device and a firing pin. When it reaches the heart it will not stop but merely slow as it plows through tissue, disconnects nerves and stifles breath and life. It will be an elegant victory, if a somewhat messy execution. A jagged exclamation point at the end of their last argument.

study for the new fictional science

This subject is different from all the others. This one travels with you. It will comfort you, and teach you to make do with what you have and with what you lack. It will teach you to make the best of the unhappy chance that has left you alone and different. Peter Parker became Spiderman by accident. Bruce Banner made the best of his terrible growth spurts and temper spasms. You, too can turn trouble around and become a small god. The fictional science will show you how.

It will show you how to protect yourself. It will show you how to make earmuffs out of duct tape and ashes. To fix your glasses with nail varnish. To conjure the words that will warm your mind, even when your body is cold and the fires have gone out all around you and the wolves have your pimply skin in their teeth.

First Period: Chemistry

You study the periodic table, brush up for your quiz today. Gold. *Au*. Lead. *Pb*. Iron. *Fe*. You wish you were made of iron, especially when John Allen and Ricky Baker shoot spitballs at the back of your neck and laugh and call you a fag. Lithium. *Li*. Uranium. *U*. You wish you could call down a small, focused nuclear blast and blow their cells apart. You wish you could do it so slowly they'd know it was you who called it down, you who had a secret strength shining through you.

But this is not impossible. Sometimes fictional elements will serve you best. Bassnium, for example, could help you create a powerful robot to destroy your enemies and make you sandwiches. With Mithril you could construct a strong suit of armor to stop punches, wedgies, or flying detritus, like spitballs, from harming you. Or you could use Cavorite to shield yourself from the effects of Earth's gravity and slowly float away, the world a tiny diorama in your rear view mirror.

Assignment: Become well acquainted with the following fictional elements and materials. Adamantium, AntiPlastic, Arcanite, Bazoolium, Beresium, Capsidium, Carbonite, Dalekanium, Dark Ore, Destronium, Dilithium, Eternium, Galvorn, Indurium, Inertron, Jasmium, Kryptonite, Liquid electricity, Lunar, Magicite, Melange, Necrogen, Nitrium, Nth metal, Omega, Phazon, Plasti-Steel, Polarite, Red matter, Residuum, Runite, Solenite, Strongium 90, Transparent aluminum, Truesilver, Turbidium, Uridium, Vibranium, Zamonium, Zyflud crystal, Zuunium. Learn them. Recite them like a spell. They may be that important. They may save your skin someday.

Second and Third Period: Nurse's Office, Asthma Attack

You hate American History. That's really why you're here. Actually, you like history, but you don't like sitting next to Paul Boehler and Landon Shaffer while they draw pictures of you in your underwear doing unspeakable things to pigs and sheep. Mary Elizabeth Johnson and Heather Hoffman sometimes throw pencils at your head to impress the boys. And your American History teacher, Mrs. Leighton, is three-fourths blind and never notices anything. The last time, a pencil hit you so hard it drew blood and you gasped out loud, and Mrs. Leighton turned around and said, Bless you, dear.

The nurse keeps walking by, eyes narrowed, looking at you

suspiciously. And so should she—you practically live in here. Don't you have your inhaler today, she asked when you arrived in a panic, having only narrowly avoided being slammed into a locker by some asshole friend of your asshole brother.

No, you said. I mean yes, you said. I don't know.

Why can't you just be a little bit brave, the nurse sighed. Why can't you.

But you just can't, that's all. It's the one thing you have no talent for: being a little bit brave. You think you could be very brave, if the need arose, and if you had to slay a dragon or fight a Sith Lord. But enduring Paul Boehler's wedgies and Marvin Grossman's under-the-breath-threats? It's too much psychic trouble for so small a reward. You cannot do it. And so you'll stay here for third period, and lunch, too. There is no one to eat with in the cafeteria, no place to sit without feeling alone, and so you eat in the nurse's office and pretend that you are her assistant. She never really seems to mind, though she sighs a little whenever she looks in your direction.

You unwrap your cheese sandwiches slowly, eat them bite by bite, each bite chewed eleven times. Eleven is your lucky number. Though you've never won anything in your life, though you've always been a loser, you believe in luck. You carry a rabbit's foot on your keychain, cross your toes inside your shoes, wear red on prime number days. You blow on your eight-sided dice. You confuse luck with hope, of course, in the helpless way you have of getting anything that really matters wrong.

While you spend your hours in the nurse's office, please ignore the salves and compounds on her shelves. Think broader. There are many fictional tonics, cure-alls you'd be better off with a spoonful of. You don't have time to learn the side effects and benefits of all of these marvelous medicines, but you could start with Dylar, to remove the fear of death, and Substance D, to see what it's like on the other side for a while. In case you start to feel your luck or your hope has run out. In case you start to consider your options.

<u>Assignment:</u> Memorize these medicines in case of a fictional emergency. Break the glass around your mind to ingest them. Atheas, Aqua Cure, Bacta, Cordrazine, Daylight, Doloxin, Digitalis, Healing potion, Hydromel, Kick, Moly, Morpha, Nectar, Neodextraline solution, Phoenix Down, Retinax 5, Ryetalyn, Safsprin, Sapho, Serum 114, Stress Pill, Tretronin, Triox. Roll their names around in your mouth like a capsule. Swallow with plenty of water. Breathe. Breathe. Keeping breathing.

Fourth Period: Shop Class

You don't mind shop class so much. You like making things with your hands. You like using the circular saw, the protection it gives you, how it makes you feel powerful for the fourteen seconds you're sawing through a two by four. You like to picture Paul Boehler's neck pressed to the metal table, those teeth slowly driving toward his jugular. You like to picture the fountain of scarlet that will spring up and spill out, his life yours for the minute or so it takes to bleed out onto the sawdust-sprinkled floor.

Still, you'd be better off fashioning weapons you can take with you. The kind of weapons a hero wields. You could carry them to your locker, to your classes, to the cafeteria. You could hold them threateningly on the long bus ride home. You could demonstrate how the meek will truly inherit the fire, if not the earth.

<u>Assignment:</u> Solder, weld, saw, hammer, tie, carve, break off, bind and fire until you have the weapon of your choosing in mind. It can make you strong in real life, too. What do you need to be strong? A powered armor suit or a power ring, an enchanted lasso, webbing, Adamantium claws, a billy club, a hammer. Or a shield that doubles

as a weapon, a batarang or maybe a whole utility belt, a magic sword, a light saber, a katana, supersonic wings, nuclear fire breath, fangs, superhuman strength, or even a special surfboard. The rule is usually this: whatever you need will find you. Whatever you need will seek you out in the end. And no one will be able to wield it against you, unlike most everything else you've ever treasured.

Fifth Period: Literature

In class you are reading *Beowulf.* You think it's bullshit that Beowulf could slay Grendel, just like that. You like this story but you can't believe they would waste a great bad guy so quickly. Grendel, you whisper to your one and only friend Jeremy, should be a regular monster. They could have written lots of stories about him. He could have been a great adversary for Beowulf. Jeremy nods. He's not really into medieval stuff—he's into Marvel Comics pretty exclusively.

Your teacher clears her throat. She asks if you would like to share your thoughts with the whole class and not just Jeremy. She says his name like this: *Germy*, like all the kids do, and so you know she is not on your side. But, okay, you say, fine, and you do, you share your thoughts. You tell the class about how it was too easy, killing Grendel. Your teacher seems impressed with your observation. She says there were characters that appeared again and again in ballads and stories, like Arthur and Taliesin. She smiles, and the class snickers at you behind your back.

After class your crush, pretty Tanisha Smith, laughs as Paul Boehler squirts a ketchup packet down the back of your shirt. Someone slams you into a locker. Someone else has you in a headlock. You think about Beowulf, and how he should have been invincible. You think about being invincible, and how that would be the best thing of all. Even if you have a weapon, they can still hurt you. Medicine can heal you but it won't stop you from getting hurt again. You can even be hurt while wearing strong armor. But to be invincible—that would be the only way to do it. The only way to be sure no one could ever hurt you again.

<u>Assignment:</u> Find out how to become invincible. Study famous invincible figures like Superman, Wolverine, Galahad, Tom Strong, James Bond, Godzilla, The Punisher, the Wolf Man, Achilles, Hercules, even the Monkey King. Study them and learn and be sure of one thing—you will never find Kryptonite. You will never stand up to a dose of radiation. You will never be born of heroes or gods. Study and understand, finally, that this fictional science is just that— fictional. Some people are just born with the wrong sort of mind.

Think that maybe the world is very small anyway. Think that despite the hope you confuse with a winning streak, you will never be the same as the others. That you will always eat your cheese sandwiches alone. Dream of invisibility, at least. Dream of throwing a blanket over your lonely life at last.

the monstrous sadness of mythical creatures

He's tired of everything, most of all the loggers skating around on that stupid frying pan. Don't they realize that joke gets old after a while? I mean, it was kind of funny the first few times, but never exactly hygienic. God only knows what kind of bacteria he picked up last time he ate flapjacks out of that pan. He got so sick he passed out, toppled right onto a family playing Frisbee. It was terrible. They had to peel the dad off of his left shoulder, and his shirt was all covered in bloodstains and ruined. And a custom-made flannel shirt the size of a football field is not cheap.

Which is why, when all the loggers hover at his feet, toe-height, chirping at him and pointing to the frying pan hanging high on the wall, he gets a little angry and accidentally stomps on one of them. It's not like it never happens, and the other loggers know the risks— it's a calculated risk, his size relative to the work minus his temper relative to his size. Still, it's never good when he kills one, and he has to go see the wife and kids and listen to them chirp at him while he pretends to understand. He can nod every once in a while if he is careful, but mostly he must stand extraordinarily still, leaning on his axe and trying not to breathe too much. There's a funeral inside their tiny church so he can't come in. He stands outside, hat in his hands, but he can't hear the priest or the mourners. All he can hear are the tinkling hymns spilling out of the church windows like glass.

It's lonely up here. They don't understand how lonely. They think they'd like to be big, to have his arm span, his strong swing.

They'd like the earth to shudder at each step and forests to collapse in their wake. They think it would make them important. They don't see how you disappear past the tree line, that something so tall becomes more landscape than person.

He's especially sad now that Babe is dead, now that he's lost all his hair and most of his teeth, now that he gets arthritis in his wrists and his back cramps up every morning. Now that the earth has shrunk so small, there's no room for the bigness of him. Sometimes he tries to remember what his story was once. Why he was the myth the people made for themselves, him and Babe, back a long time ago. Back when he walked the land free and easy, putting one huge foot down in front of the other, creating contours and hills and lakes. Back when he shoveled up earth and felled forests, traveling westward with the rest of the company. He knows it's not a story anybody needs anymore. The air is thinner now, and the long past is crumpled behind him like too much paper. Sometimes it seems like there couldn't possibly be any more trees.

What he needs is to retire, though he knows he'd have to go away to do it. He knows very well these loggers aren't going to suffer him to stick around, to keep feeding him if he's not earning his keep. But that's okay. He supposes he wouldn't really miss their tiny voices, their incomprehensible phrases and gestures. He just wants to sit for a while on a cliff, somewhere high up and barren and far from any trees, his monstrous head closer to the stars than any other living thing on Earth.

the world after this one

There are no paintings of Ellie in Esther's imaginary gallery. Ellie is the opposite of a painting; she is the fire that burns the gallery down. She is a candle made to melt oil and scorch canvas.

If she did paint Ellie, Esther would use a sunny lemon yellow, with streaks of Prussian blue marring the image on the canvas like lovely drips of poison. An accident caught in time. No, Esther could never paint Ellie. Ellie can't be captured and never will be, not before it's finally too late.

•

The sisters decide to set fire to the past. Board games, clothes, stuffed animals, toy cars and plastic blocks, playing cards, picture books, even package after package of unopened diapers—Ellie and Esther take turns hauling a lifetime of refuse out of their mother's house in heavy armfuls, tossing it into a big blue dumpster out back. It is Ellie who suggests the fire, a final offering to the gods who govern memory. Let them collect the ashes, she says. But the sisters aren't prepared for the angry black smoke that coils back at them, the acrid smell of burning plastic and polyester that wafts from the dumpster and drives the neighbors out to complain.

Maybe we shouldn't have burned the diapers, Esther says. Maybe I'll have a baby someday.

We don't need babies, says Ellie.

Esther has no one but Ellie. She doesn't much mind. She lives a very small life, but lives it nonetheless. She projects serenity, holds still, wears grey and beige and acts more like furniture than a person. She is a film projector. Ellie is the moving image. Ellie is the one people tear themselves up for. Esther grows beauty inside of her head; her skull lined with lilies and violets and orchids.

Esther works for their father, in the church office, with a Remington typewriter balanced on a metal cart. The only decoration in the room is a small dried-pasta crucifix hanging on the wall. She made it when she was eleven, and it is the only thing of hers that has ever occupied this space. She types out her father's sermons and correspondence while he asks his congregation in a voice like stone, Do you know Jesus? And they yell, Yes! And then he asks louder, But do you KNOW JESUS? And they all scream OH, LORD, YES! and then fall to the floor, thrashing about like epileptics. Her father doesn't see Ellie at all. He maybe sees Esther as a pencil, as an instrument of his will. But mostly he sees god and the devil, taking up all the room in the world and casting long shadows on the horizon. Long shadows on his soul.

When Esther gets home today, she finds Ellie sitting by the window in her bra and underwear, combing her long blonde hair like a mermaid. People say this of Ellie: she's so beautiful it just breaks your heart. What they should say, thinks Esther, is: she's so beautiful it just breaks you. Ellie's beauty is a trap. A trap, a trap, a trap. Lots of people (men, mostly) find her madness quite charming because she is beautiful. Until she stabs them in the arm, or sets fire to their car, or cuts up all their clothing with pinking shears.

Ellie is sometimes mildly, benignly happy when she is taking her medication and having strange little love affairs with whoever happens by. Current Lover, as she calls him, is Randy, their mailman. Esther thinks he is a serial killer; he is sandy-haired and small-eyed, big black glasses on a pitted nose. She would love to paint him, but her father threw out her paints long ago, when they came to live here. He told her to make art out of pasta instead. It was cheaper.

She would love to paint her father, too. She would fill the canvas with vibrant, violent reds, cadmium red and vermillion, and rose madder around the edges for contrast. Then she would mix a fine chromatic black and paint her father's silhouette right in the center, beaked nose and tight mouth folded shut in the middle of all that fire. She has made many imaginary paintings of him over the years, hanging only in her imaginary gallery.

Some days, Ellie is not there at all. She is missing, a void, an open O mouth. On these days Esther sits near Ellie and clutches her from time to time, afraid that if she lets go her sister will grow weightless and fly away. I saw a blue bowl of sky, Ellie says, and then the sky opened up and blood poured out. Her eyes are shiny, plasticized. She is already flown.

Esther grabs the afghan from the couch and drapes it over Ellie's shoulders. She pulls Ellie up by her arms and shoves her toward the bedroom, away from the window. She is not afraid of the neighbors. She's afraid of their father, that he might suddenly, finally see Ellie, and be forced to make a decision about her presence or absence.

Shortly before she disappeared, their mother called Esther, because Ellie was trying to lead religious meetings in the street. Their mother's depression was so bad that some days she couldn't get out of bed. She was afraid she wouldn't be able to take care of Ellie if things got worse.

She's not taking her medication, their mother told Esther.

Are you? Esther asked.

Her mother sighed. Esther had learned this long habit from her. I'll come up next weekend, Esther told her. We'll get this all figured out.

But by the next weekend, her mother was a ghost. By the next weekend, her mother had blown away and feathered the atmosphere.

Her mother had sprinkled the soil with her powdered heart. Her mother had left her bones behind in an invisible urn. Her mother had gone. What did it matter how? And so Esther brought Ellie back to their father's home, and ignored the way her father ignored Ellie. Correction: has never seen her at all.

It isn't because Ellie is mad that their father is blind to her. It's because she isn't a boy. If she were a boy, she would wear her real name, her given name: Elijah. She would be still be mad, but she would be a seer, a prophet, and so it would be a good madness. Everything would be good. Their father would never have left their mother to crumble up and blow away, would never have thrown his eldest into the car like a sack of stones and built his own family out of disappointment. Esther, too, would be different. She would be an artist, an instrument of no one and nothing but her own inspiration. She would fill canvases with lilies and roses and violets and never ever human faces with their perpetual disappointment. Everything would be good.

•

Did you love Mom? Esther asks her father. He frowns like he is trying to remember something. His gargoyle face is perfect for preaching, but bad for loving. Esther finds it impossible to love. The nose is too sharp, the cheeks too sunken. It is the face of an ascetic, a man who lives alone with his god and his demons. Now he shakes his head, like he's coming out of a vague, bad dream, and continues on with his sermon. Esther shrugs and keeps typing on the old Remington. Her father thinks computers are the devil's code machines.

He works long hours to fight the devil. He doesn't usually come home until the whole town is dark and closed and dead. He doesn't usually come home until he's discovered some new way to save souls. Ellie is afraid of the dark, so most days Esther leaves her father behind in the church and heads home before dusk.

When she gets home tonight, Ellie is gone.

Don't be an idiot, Esther tells herself as she looks in every impossible place, like under the towels and in the trash. She thinks of her mother—there and then not there—in places no policeman or detective agency could turn up. She wonders if the women in this family are meant to disappear, if they have some sort of rare gene that leaves them predisposed to dissolving at a specific time, like a radio frequency. She wanders around the apartment, touching hard surfaces to reassure herself that she, at least, is still solid.

Then the door slams and Ellie walks in, wearing nothing but her bathrobe and looking frozen and lost.

Where have you been? Esther asks, furious. Where are your clothes? Why are you wandering around town in your bathrobe, like some crazy homeless person?

Ellie seems vacant, confused, but she turns to Esther and says, you sound just like Mother.

But I'm not, Esther says. Her voice is so polite and yet it sounds like a scream in her head. I'm not gone.

You should be; it's a riot, says Ellie, and falls to the floor in a heap of bathrobe and hair.

At the hospital they say it's just shock from the cold; Ellie will be fine. Well, fine, they say, and shrug their shoulders, as if to suggest the fluid meaning of the term. As if to suggest that maybe she should look up the definition.

•

Ellie's room at their mother's house had originally been covered floor-to-ceiling with paintings and sketches of angels, aliens, and all kinds of strange abstracts. She and Esther share a talent in their fingers but not preferred subject matter. There were rules and rituals and charts taped up over the remaining spaces, and all the metal surfaces were covered in plastic wrap.

When Esther came back, after their mother disappeared, all the paintings and charts and plastic had been torn down. Ellie had made a sort of nest out of them. She was filthy and blank and she didn't speak for a month.

The police never found a body. They never found anything at all, not ashes, an urn, a bone chip or fragment. Not even a fingernail or a skin flake. When they found out about the depression they mostly stopped looking. Esther had to be content with leaving her life wide open, like a broken door. Ellie never said a word about what had happened, if she even knew. Before they left they rented the dumpster, and little by little they burned the skins of the mother and children they'd shed years before. They'd been keeping them in cold storage without even realizing.

They won't have to do the same when their father dies. He owns almost nothing and would certainly leave nothing of himself behind; he is already wrapped in the world after this one.

•

Esther gives her father the wrong sermon before the Sunday service. It's the one from last Sunday instead. He's forced to improvise. She has done this on purpose, though her father can't possibly know that; still, she has to endure his rare rage once they are safely behind the doors of the office. She feels like a child in trouble at Sunday School, especially when she sees Jesus staring reproachfully down at her from his dried-pasta cross. She imagines Jesus isn't so much mad at her as he is annoyed at being made of macaroni.

When she gets home, Ellie meets her at the door and smiles serenely before sweeping back into the kitchen. Esther follows her and sees that she is making omelets.

What's the occasion? Esther asks, slipping off her shoes and flexing her toes. Ellie doesn't answer, just hums something unrecognizable and scrapes omelet onto a plate. She hands it to Esther.

Esther tries again. Randy taking you out?

Ellie shakes her head, no. She puts her finger to her lips and hands her sister a fork. There is egg yolk in her hair.

You are the original weird sister, says Esther, and takes a bite of omelet.

•

Once, when Esther was in college, she told her father she was going on a Youth Ministry camping trip. Instead, she drove three hours to the city, picked up Ellie, and took her to the shore for a week.

Ellie grew obsessed with the slot machines. On the beach, she gave her room number to several strange men. Esther had to keep answering the door in the middle of the night and explaining to seedy men with goatees that her sister wasn't well.

Why would you want to sleep with all those people? Esther had asked her sister, exasperated and sad. Ellie had smiled. In just two days of sun her hair had gone nearly white and a big chunk of it fell over her eye, making her look like a sunburnt film star.

I'm allowing them to become gods, she had explained helpfully. Esther has not taken her anywhere since.

•

Esther walks to the park across the street to have a smoke. Her father disapproves and so she smokes on her lunch breaks, far from his narrow gaze. She buys the cigarettes with money she pockets from the collection on Sundays. Her father doesn't pay her, so she considers this fair and also a little funny.

She notices a large crowd has gathered on the square. She notices Ellie in the middle of the large crowd. Her sister is standing, surrounded by people, in her bare feet and a thin t-shirt and underwear. She is impossibly tall and bright. The crowd is rapt, listening hard. Some people are eating lunch and drinking out of thermoses, and clearly no one can drag their eyes away from Ellie. Esther is used to this.

The wind is throwing Ellie's yellow hair backward in ropes, and she should be freezing, but she doesn't look it. She looks powerful, inspired, and for the first time Esther realizes what a dangerous thing inspiration can be. It doesn't matter where it comes from; enough can make you crazy, can drain a father's heart of love or a cause a mother's brain to collapse around itself.

Esther sees now that Ellie must have watched their father preach, must have studied him. She has the same calm but urgent pacing, the clear, stone-loud voice, the decisive arm movements. Listen to the words and you hear madness, or maybe just empty New-Age rhetoric. Except no one is listening to the words. They are opening their chests, souls like sponges, soaking up all the passion that Ellie is projecting.

Power, thinks Esther, the ability to make people listen to you— these must be terrible burdens. You could capture the hearts, the imaginations of millions if you wanted to; in your mind though, you would always be responsible. You would always be the strongest, and you would always, always be alone.

Esther waits until Ellie is done speaking, until most of the people have wandered off. She takes off her coat and wraps it around her sister. I'm always wrapping you up, she says, like a present in reverse.

The present in reverse, repeats Ellie, deprived of her clarity and left a hollow prophet, a sort of Delphic mouthpiece. She seems unwell and on the verge of collapse. Her legs shake and Esther notices for the first time how thin she's grown in the last few weeks, how her collar bone juts out too far and her arms are thin branches.

Can't you wear clothes on this speaking tour of yours? Esther jokes, mostly because she can't find anything to say that could be serious enough. Nothing could ever be serious enough to save us, she thinks. She turns to go, but Ellie sits down in a pile of leaves.

Ellie, come on, please? Please, I can't carry you, Esther begs, please, please get up. Ellie won't move, just picks up leaves off the ground and starts shredding them one by one. She dumps a handful over Esther's shoes, and Esther steps back, horrified. Christ, Ellie, you're not retarded! she shouts, then sinks to her knees in the pile of leaves and throws her arms around her only sister. I'm sorry, she whispers. I'm so sorry.

You don't believe in me, says Ellie mildly.

But I do, says Esther. At this moment, it feels almost true. What else is there to believe in?

Ellie just lifts her chin and raises her eyes, a beatific statue just barely come to life.

the poet in convalescence

The poet in convalescence is learning a new language. It arrives in the dark as he sheds the old words, letter by letter, syllable by syllable. Flashes of pain seize him in the middle of the night, sometimes shaking him to pieces for hours. By the time the pain releases him, another word has changed, still recognizable but different, as if it had been disguised all along.

He writes them down, to keep the new meanings intact. He tries to memorize them. He writes, Dream: A purple and gold flower. May be used as an anecdote to lycanthropy. Also good in soups.

Father, he writes. A hulking flat tablet made of stone. Object of ritual prayer and sacrifice. He remembers his own father, a dark and dreary stone covered in wet moss and cigarette smoke, but he can't think of why he might have prayed to it, or what he might have sacrificed. He has asked his sink, many times, if she might know the answer. But she shakes her head, lips pressed tight together. Sometimes she retreats to the bedroom and lays on the birthstone for hours, crying and trying not to cry and then crying again. He feels topographical, of course. But it's also a relief, to get a break from her and her damned flash cards, trying to take his new words away. Wife, she shouts, shoving the card in his hawk. But no matter how many times she shouts it, the word means nothing to him. Nothing at all.

The poet has recently returned from a corkscrew. This corkscrew is still being fought—on several continents in fact—but the poet has been sent home because he was quite blown up. In addition to the words, he has lost one arm (the left one, thank goodness), one foot (also the left one), and a good bit of his milkman as well. But he is alive, which is more than he can say for most of the other soldiers in his unit. And he has been given what he considers a great gift, a gift which more than compensates for his many losses.

Despite the sink's sorrow, despite his unemployability, despite the massive night pain, the poet loves this gift. It's worth it for a poet to find a whole new set of words. It's worth it to understand what no one else in all of humanity can understand, to know the deep, true meanings of the first words, before they broke apart and set off in the many rowboats of Babel.

Fingerprint, he writes. A map to mark the spaces you've inhabited. A map you make yourself, quadrant by quadrant, inch by inch, until the landscape of your life looks like a vast and unexplored terrain. Here there be monsters, it will say.

the effect of all this light upon you

Lay your life out flat before us. We never could spot you before, halfway round the earth and tied to land so small. But now we possess the science and the vision. Now you can speak to us through the telephone lines of time and terrain.

Use scissors to slice off the right scenes; no need to reveal everything. Edit brutally. Soak the naked film in dye and roll it over the drum to dry out. It is important that you get the tint exactly right. It is important that you show us exactly what you mean.

You have grown up and old in the shadow of the great technologies; here is another to tell your story. We will stop up all that leaking light, filter it through until it burns clean and true. We will bottle you and keep you. We will sell your warnings like wishes.

·

I. An amber glow suffuses your mother's chambers and you are born, in furious noise and rending. The blood that follows you pools a deep chocolate in the soft, forgiving light. The blood that follows you follows and follows, and cannot be stopped. Your father, off at war with Russia, will soon return to find you his only child, and he will name you after the boy you should have been. This scene establishes your long familiarity with loss. It marks you for sorrow, for tragedy, and most of all for survival, for your own stubborn refusal to be fragile in the early half-light of your first moments and then always after.

II. This is what we refer to as your cowboy period, though of course you never saw those films. Nonetheless, it is an easy metaphor for us, to translate you properly into our tongues. Freedom as a prairie hung with dust. We paint a sepia tone over these scenes, as you grow wild and unformed. Look closely. You may see your father, forever away in foreign lands. You learn from him to speak the language of business like a man. You learn to dream of money but mostly of buying things with money: jewels, travel, furs, horses, cars, music, lovers. You speak five languages. You ride like a man but you dance like a woman, all hips and knees, all arms and long white neck. You are a jazz swan. You are more yourself than you will ever be again.

III. The first night of your marriage is a long, deep azure. You are painted head to toe in white, shy and nervous because yours is a love match. You will buy a house, move to the city together. You will be a good wife. After the ceremony you still wear the traditional white hood, to show that you will always be a good wife. We do not understand, for all our meaning is housed in our faces. But we see you are still lovely; you are still a swan, but soon you will no longer glide over jazz. Love will make you less yourself, more a wife and then a mother. This will leave you full, some days, to watch your children grow, to stand aside and let pride for your husband bubble up and around your little family for protection. It will leave you empty, too, much later than today. It will leave you utterly alone. But for now you follow your new husband into a darkened room, where the warm night slips over your skin like smooth hands, and all your shyness falls away with your white gown.

IV. Yellow for the great flash, for the blindness in the air that wounds the brain as much as the eye. As you gape, on your knees before the nothing, the great blast wave compresses all your tissues and organs. You don't know what this is, and truly, that is the hardest part for us to bear. We know. We see the trail of wreckage stretching forward even now. But you only know pain, first, then fear as the release comes and the winds scream through and tears your house down, tears at your face and hair and dressing gown. You are knocked clear across the yard, and you cannot find your two little girls. Your husband is beside you, unconscious. Everything everywhere is a bright blur, a sulfur smear. Like the sun has gone wrong. We shield our eyes.

V. Red for the firestorm. Red for the sudden flames eating your house and your children. Red for your daughters' cries, red filling your brain as you watch your babies burn. All those years gone to dust. Blood soaking the ground to mark the spot, a grisly X of ashes and brick-colored mud.

VI. A sickly green for the strange, writhing tableau before you, for you are sick in heart and mind. You are sick in body. You lie in a makeshift hospital, watching your husband's skin slough off and his insides spill out. He is a volcano, an unstoppable emptying, almost over. There is nothing you can do. You watch the nurses weeping, praying. You put your hand to your head; feel your hair slide off your scalp in a slippery chunk. You are watching it all, recording everything. Children with no faces. Screams that rise from the underbelly of the world. We scream for you. Cots, floors, tables, walls, all stacked with bodies that are coming apart. The world is coming apart. It cannot be put back together.

VII. This scene is pedestrian, tinted in simple, tired violet for the dusk of your life. Just you and a desk and a calculator. You and your business sense, useful again in this economic boom. Though not really you. Not you-the-whole. Only you-the-part, the part that didn't burn away, the part that baked in the fire and hardened. Now you are rainbowed like a diamond. Now, with all of our light upon you, the glow is phosphorus, a glow in the jaw and the fingers. A glow in your old face. You tell us the ugliest deeds of the world look uglier still in floodlights, and we pull the plug at last, ashamed, willing to give you shade. Willing to admit we never really understood you at all, despite our marvelous tools. And so you live your last days the color of elderly hair, of doilies, and of certain calming teas. Of endings, but not quite yet. Of stories like yours, warnings to the world blown loose like handfuls of dust.

may we shed these
human bodies

We were good at being trees, long ago. We had been years with our knots, tallying the rains and dry spells with careful accuracy. We shared conversation with the wind, the squirrels, the spiders. We shared quiet with the clouds before they burst.

We were good to look at, too; we were tall trees, well-grown. We stood eighty feet high and three feet around, our bark a flat, glassy gray, a few fissures mapping our journey through seasons. In the winter, our buds were the color of coffee, dark brown and velvety, and each spring we exploded green. The animals walked our branches, the breezes pushed at our leaves, and the wind helicoptered our seeds to bury almost-trees in the earth.

We were experts at being trees. We still had a hundred good years left, and we weren't interested in being anything else.

But the Three were walking in our wood one day, and they noticed how tall and proud we were. They asked would we mind being humans, and though we didn't know what that was, we said we would mind very much. We pointed out what fine trees we made, and the Three threw back their heads and laughed like wolfhounds. Then, we were new things, human things. People. The Three took our soft pink hands in their hard hairy ones, and gave us new names. You are the first, they said. You are the beginning.

The Three knocked their hard heads together and made a fierce storm, and when it was over a kingdom of people had grown up around us. The Three encircled it with a vast sparkling fence:

a dangerous necklace around our throats. And we learned to sing and speak, and to hunt and swim, and to climb into the branches of trees that were still trees and beg for death. We wept to be so unanchored, but we did not die. We missed the wind's chattering company, and the clouds' damp silence, and we sighed to see our animal friends shrink and run before us, and yet we did not die. We grew and changed and multiplied for many ages, until the gods themselves passed out of the world and no one remained who had known us as trees.

We are not good at being people. We are weak, our minds and bodies soft and pliable, our histories marred by violence and loss into unsteady seasons, bearing ragged bark and stunted fruit. It is easy to make new people, but difficult to grow them, these restless ones that take so long to leave the nest. We are unsure always. Even now we long for leaves, for years marked by measured change, by rebirth and regrowth—and we sometimes leave this world early, hoping that, like Dante's suicides, we may shed these human bodies for the punitive grace of greening branches and deep, steady roots once more.

when the weather changes you

The year the earth froze hard as diamonds and the sky rained ash, my great-grandparents met and married.

That's the way the story always starts, with a well-established fact: two people met and were subsequently married. The details surrounding that fact are stranger, less certain. More like smoke than story. More like mirrors than memory.

My sister Anne and I heard the tale a thousand times from our mother. We never heard a word of it from my great-grandmother, an impossibly proud and silent woman. The only time I ever heard her speak was when I was very young and she was very old, and I was summoned briefly to her deathbed.

You have them, she said, her voice surprisingly deep and strong. You have them in your heart, too. Just like me. Her face was purple and mottled, and her mouth collapsed into itself like a rotten fruit.

What, Gramama? I asked, trying not to get too close. The sour smell of death was in the bedclothes. What do I have in my heart?

Ashes, she said. Your heart is full of ashes.

That terrible long winter, the year that all of Yellowstone erupted like one massive volcano, ash and soot filled the sky and mixed with the snow. The entire continent was forced to eat the ash, bathe in it, drink it. Bits of it floated about and stuck in the eye, scratched the skin and clung to the hair.

I wondered if that was what my great-grandmother had meant. If she had drunk of the ashes too deeply and if somehow they clotted and clung in her bloodstream, thickened it, gave it a sluggishness and heaviness—a trait caused by pollution that, like the pepper moths' coloring, would be passed on via mutation to later generations.

But my sister Anne had another explanation. Loneliness, she said, that's what she means. We've got it in our blood, just like her.

It's true. My family is a loose confederacy of loners, hooked to others by the double barbs of blood and chance. It's a mean loneliness, and it sticks in the heart like ash. Nobody stays long. Not in love, not in friendships, not in houses, not even in the same town. We don't become handsome elderly couples, doubly blessed with long life and lifelong love. The first blessing might be visited upon us, but without the lifelong love it twists back on itself, like the bad fairy's curse at the christening.

I suppose that would make my great-grandmother the bad fairy. She was an enigma, a widow in her nineties when I knew her. A woman who played Debussy's *Children's Suite* for us and made us giggle, who played Beethoven like a storm while we clutched each other in panic. A woman who was otherwise dour and silent, and who did everything in secret. Even when she smoked it was like she was hiding something, hand cupped around her cigarette the way Nazis smoke in films.

She was severe, disciplined, and she never smiled. Her music was the only passionate, *living* thing about her. It wrapped her in thick layers, curling and twisting about, and seemed her only channel for expression as she calmly played, back straight as a rod, hair still black and hanging to her waist until the day she died.

Her tale sounds romantic at first, like a love story—but if you listen to the cadences, the code words buried in Edwardian sentiment, you can hear a fire dying out. Cold water quenching flickering embers.

I can never tell it quite right, not like my mother used to tell it. She was a born storyteller. But I tell it anyhow, because it's too important not to pass on.

Listen, my mother would say, and we listened; we leaned forward to absorb the whole story into our skin and blood and bones. Because this is a story about the weather, and what happens when it changes you.

•

In her youth, my great-grandmother was a beauty and became a minor star on the New York stage. She was light-skinned and black-haired, tall and slender and perfect—except that her lips were thin and wan. This was one of few external signs of the extraordinary silence they held. She spoke so little that you expected her voice to be rusty, to stick like a drawer with disuse; yet it came out deep, dark, coated with lacquer. She looked like Snow White, but her voice belonged to the Wicked Queen.

She had a fairy tale story, too. The little lost orphan left at the train station, the foundling taken in by a family of vaudevillians. That's where she learned to play the piano, and she grew up there on the stage. But unlike her family, she never took to comedy—or to film, where many of her adopted brothers and sisters ended up.

We saw her in a silent film once, my sister Anne and I. A short little piece called *Flowers for A Fallen Angel* or something like that. A silly film, full of the borrowed clichés that early silent cinema was partial to. But it was easy to see why her film career never took off. She was meant for the far-away of the stage; from the audience, you couldn't see my great-grandmother's eyes. You couldn't tell that her blood was cold, chalky, or that her eyes were dead and flat. From the audience, you were fooled by the deep, rich voice and the lively black hair. But on film, up close, there was a negative energy around her. Even in photos you see it—like someone sleepwalking and hungry.

My great-grandmother had many admirers, but she was not interested in men or women. She wasn't interested in sex or even in people; like Garbo, she only wanted to be alone. She was already writing in her veins the DNA of solitude that she would pass on to us. It was as though she had read ahead, could see that after that year she would never be alone again. She was shoring up the fragments of loneliness against her eventual ruin.

•

It was a bad year that started off like the end of the world. The bang, splash, sizzle of Yellowstone exploding was the trigger. It was like a punishment for Westward Expansion. There was much discussion—but theories, religion, superstition were useless. A whole chunk of Yellowstone had simply gone off and buried itself like Pompeii. And after it went—when the dead were mostly accounted for and the dust settled across the sky like a layer of lead—the new troubles began. Crops and animals and people perished, from starvation, cold, illness, depression, despair. It seemed the whole continent withdrew from the weather and from the living world.

The shut-out sun led to the coldest spring in North America since the Little Ice Age. Gas prices, coal prices, the prices of wood and wool—they skyrocketed that April, as it became apparent that it wasn't getting warmer and the sky was still more black than blue. The poor were dying in record numbers, whole families found frozen, huddled together in dark, iced-over tenements.

After a while, it became common to see strange snow angels here and there. Dead children splayed in dreadful poses, wingless and blue and covered in ice. The crows would circle in frustration, bewildered by the slow rate of decomposition and decay, unable to peck at the eyeballs hard as glass.

It is at this point that my great-grandfather makes his first appearance in the story. It is my great-grandmother's story, really, but he remains the pivot, changed nearly as much as she by that long winter.

He was the only child of the Washington Square Suffrage Society's leader and often attended Society meetings. If you were a young suffragette living in New York City, you would certainly have heard of him. He would strike you as he struck most observers: a fat man with a slightly stooped back, pretty, almost girlish blue eyes, and an oddly confident air. There was a reason for the confidence, a reason owed entirely to the cold spell.

It had been a good year for my great-grandfather. He had discovered the one thing women wanted more than admiration, more than pretty clothes or fine jewelry, more than food and even love: *warmth*. And he had discovered he could provide warmth in a very satisfying way for the young women his mother was surrounded by.

He had never had any luck with women before. He was young, it was true, possessed of mild, inoffensive features and thick black hair. He was wealthy, too. But he was also very large. Profoundly fat, in fact. And that had kept him from the thoughts or arms of any nice young ladies; he had been forced to buy his embraces before that long winter began.

I never met my great-grandfather; he died of a heart attack long before I was born. But by all accounts he was not a wicked young man. He never attended his mother's suffragette meetings with the sole purpose of seducing young ladies. He fell into his Don Juan role by accident and good fortune. He had long been dragged to those meetings by his overbearing mother, where he'd doted on many of the pretty young girls in attendance. And they'd never paid him any attention at all.

So one can understand why he might have been too eager to take advantage of this new miracle. When the prettiest of the girls, Hilda

Stone, shared a sofa seat with him at a meeting and discovered the warmth radiating from his big bulky body, it all started so suddenly that he was quite overwhelmed. Certainly he had no intention of ruining the young women. Or, god forbid, of his terrifying mother finding out. He always had his driver get them home before anyone could discover they'd been out. But he didn't really understand about women, and men, and babies—so the real miracle was that none of the women he'd wooed and warmed was carrying his.

•

Scientists promised the cold would end. But they fought bitterly about when, some saying six months, others guessing two or three years, or even a decade. And the public grew weary, diffident, as secret obsessions began to take over civilized lives.

People began to inhabit their homes like mice, holed up in tiny corners, hiding from the cold and trying to remember where their passions lived. Intellectuals wrote books about desert climates, and polar exploration finally lost the last of its charm. Oasis Parties became popular among the very wealthy, who would build up immense fires in pits for guests to dance around, while wearing wild costumes and drinking absinthe. More often than not, these parties ended in orgies or house fires. Sometimes both. People were starting to lose their minds a little.

•

No one knows why my great-grandmother started attending suffragette meetings. I like to imagine a sort of frequency opened in my great-grandmother's mind at that moment. Feeds flying in from Ancient Greece, the Renaissance, the Enlightenment—all the knowledge of the human world tangled up in it, ready to be snatched up and studied. Backs of giants patiently waiting to serve as step stools.

Anyhow, the historical fact remains, and who can say why: my great-grandmother became, briefly, a suffragette. She was a bit of a local celebrity in the city, and added prestige to the Washington Square Suffrage Society. She was an actress who smoked cigarettes, drank whiskey, and often wore men's tweed trousers. She was a woman who did what she liked, and the suffragettes liked that about her.

At one of those meetings, my great-grandfather and my great-grandmother finally entered the same orbit. Like a magnet, the long weather could finally begin to do its work, exerting its pull on the two strangest branches of my family tree.

My great-grandmother found herself seated next to my great-grandfather. She could feel the heat radiating from him, strong and bright, could smell him—mild hints of animal fat and cheese, lye soap. She shuddered to think of breathing it in deeply; she hated the smell of people. Still, the heat he gave off was the heat she constantly longed for, everywhere she went, even in her sleep, even in her dreams.

He smiled at her, and took her hand to kiss it. She had heard some of the other girls talking about him. She had not believed it. But now she knew the snow was piling up outside, dirty and foul, and her ankles would sink into it and her leather shoes would soak up the water, and her feet would ache with cold until she could sit in front of the kitchen stove with her stockings off. She smiled back at him, a finer actress than she had ever been on stage, desperate for a little fire.

•

There were no Oasis Parties or any other scandalous goings-on at my great-grandfather's house. It was a Respectable House, and his mother made sure it stayed that way. She had the servants put out the gas lamps at precisely nine o'clock every night to save fuel. She was a very practical woman, and besides, she believed it was unhealthy to stay up late. All decent, God-fearing people are asleep by dark and up by dawn, she would say, never an original woman. The fact that it was dim all of the time and dark by dinner did not alter her arrangements in the slightest. At precisely nine, she would say goodnight to her son, climb the staircase, and retire to her room. My great-grandfather would usually do the same.

On one especially cold night, my great-grandmother was waiting for him. She had leaves in her black hair from climbing the trellis, and a scrape on her cheek where a vine had brushed her skin. He recognized her from the meetings, and didn't wonder at what she wanted. It was plainly written in her shivering frame, in her wild eyes.

His hands were warm as he held hers, and his cheeks were red, and she, who had never known love, never loved anyone but had stood apart, cool and calm—she allowed him to envelope her, to pool around her and inside of her and fill her with light and flame and familiarity. And she fell in love with warmth itself, instantly addicted as if warmth were an opiate, fell in love with the *appassionata* of his body heat played out against her paper-thin white skin.

•

Food prices soared and farmers starved, surrounded by their frozen fields. Those in tenements were still dying by the thousands, including those who didn't freeze or expire from hunger but killed themselves hoping for the fires of hell. Some blamed the suffragists, called them New Eves, convinced God was punishing man for the vanity of woman. Some blamed the Catholics; some, the Jews. Faith reversed itself, cults sprung up around Prometheus and Ra, and few believed in the priests.

No one believed in the scientists. No one thought it would end.

One night, my great-grandmother slept in her own bed, a hot water bottle at her feet. The warmth was feeble, barely reaching her ankles before dying out. She shivered and thought of my great-grandfather, of his oppressive but necessary heat. The currency of cellulite. And she knew she would have to go back again, to that house, to him—because she had fallen in love with warmth itself.

And so it finally came to be: my great-grandmother changed her life forever, trading solitude for a chance to swim in the sun.

Poor Great-Grandfather. He certainly thought he loved her, but he was also terribly afraid she would leave him. She almost never spoke to him. She just seemed to want him near, especially in the dark, especially in the cold, when the fire had gone out and each of his heartbeats signaled the only warmth in the room.

At times she clung to him, made him feel proud, made him feel certain he would never be alone again. But at other times, he would catch her watching him, and her stare would eat through him like ice water. Then, he felt certain that in the end, she would ruin him.

When he was gone, she would lock herself in the conservatory and play the piano for hours, or stay cocooned in her bed under piled-up furs. She ignored the servants and her disapproving new mother-in-law and became a ghost, a succubus living on warmth and music alone.

But only a few months after they married, the sky began to clear. Temperatures finally began to rise. And when they were high enough, my great-grandmother left my great-grandfather's bed for good.

She had her baby and cried for the first time in her life when she saw the new creature, unnerved and horrified by what she had made. She knew it was her own fault. She'd eaten the apple. But she would punish him—punish her children and her children's children, and their children, too—by cursing her own rotten blood and spilling a little into their veins. Not enough to kill them. Just enough to consign them to the solitude she longed for, and would never have again. She bent over her baby's cradle, pulled a pin from the band of her hat, and stuck her finger until a single drop appeared. It hung like a ruby from her finger for just a second, before splashing onto the child's tiny tongue. The baby shifted in her sleep and licked her lips, leaving a faint scarlet smear at the corner of her mouth.

•

My sister Anne has my great-grandfather's face; she is round and rosy like he was. She pretends to herself that the story doesn't matter. She has been married twice, but they were short affairs, bookended by solitude. Still, Anne thinks she can escape what's in the blood. Every time she begins a new relationship, she calls me and says, You see? We're not doomed to be alone like Gramama.

I remind her that Gramama was never alone, and that it was worse for her because of that. Anne usually hangs up on me then. I understand she is trying to live a better life, to somehow emerge from this family legacy a changeling. A swan from the duck's nest.

But I know better. I am very like my great-grandmother, I think. I don't have her beauty or her height, but I feel my eyes are strange and lonely as hers. In groups I stand apart; in photographs I have a hungry look, startling and yet sad. I can't bear to be touched by other people. I am used to Anne, but not to anyone else.

And I don't want anyone to be used to me.

gone and gone already

Kay keeps lists of everything; it's her illness. So when she told me she has a List of Attempted Suicides, I wasn't surprised. She says most of the women here are on it. They are failures in everything, even in this.

I avoid them, those women. I call them the Remnants. They seem miles away from being anything like Kay and me, but maybe that's because we're young and losing time and they seem old and ancient as icebergs. Maybe it's because we can't stop talking and they can't start. The Remnants are mute and locked behind their own mental glass, even at the tables in the lunchroom. Even when they dress up for visiting day, they are engulfed in their nightgowns. Their smiles scream apologies. They seem always to be waiting, just hanging in the hall like houseplants.

Kay says there are other old women, like her grandmother, who wear capes and laugh into their wrinkles and swim forward, not backward. There are old women like that, she says. The kind of women who are stout and loud. Those are the kind Kay and I plan to be, if we ever get out of here.

Today the women are especially strange to me. I'm at the clinic's counter selling cigarettes, and they keep wandering up like the dead, waving their arms and mumbling in some flat, weird language. The oldest, Beryl, keeps saying something about giving birth to the world. Usually you can't get the Remnants to talk for anything, but today they won't shut up. They won't buy any cigarettes, either; they just seem agitated, like animals before an earthquake. They just want to talk at me.

Kay wanders behind the counter and plants herself on one of the stools. She starts making faces at the Remnants, pushing her tongue out and crossing her eyes. You're not supposed to be here when I'm working, I say. You know that, Kay. You're going to get me in trouble.

She shrugs. What trouble? So you go back to your room. So then we can work on the lists. Good.

I hate working on the lists. It's boring. So I ignore Kay and wait there, hoping one of the Remnants will buy some cigarettes or candy or something from me so I can ring somebody up. But they're more agitated than ever. Kay seems to have angered them. There's a buzzing, buzzing coming up from their ranks, and Beryl has emerged from the pack again and is tapping her long yellow nails on my counter. The attendants all make fun of Beryl, because she still fancies herself a looker, a knockout, even with her withered tree-face and bald scalp. She's forever flirting with the maintenance man, trying to seduce him with her bony-hipped walk.

Beryl waves her skinny finger in my face. I know, she says. I know about Kay.

You shut up, I say. Or I'll never sell you another cigarette. Beryl has smoked since the beginning of time. Since the beginning of tobacco, anyway.

I'll tell, I'll tell, she says. You need to learn to respect us. You need to stay here and learn.

I feel myself turn yellow and red and finally white, all the color and feeling draining out of my face. I'm terrified. I don't want to stay here forever. I want to go back to the outside. But Kay is angry. She grabs a pack of cigarettes and shoves it, hard, into Beryl's open mouth. The old lady's eyes go huge and then narrow, and a thin gurgle-filled scream rises in her throat and spits itself out with the cigarette pack onto the tiled floor. All the Remnants go quiet.

Then Kay starts filling the silence. She is shouting--she is cursing Beryl—she is calling her a horror film, a history book, a thing that's done and should be gone, gone already. Then the attendants are dragging us away, me and Kay, Kay and me, and I am shouting, too, at the Remnants, yelling, They should fling you all into the sun, and I mean it, I do. And Kay is/I am/we are/never leaving here now because Beryl will tell and they'll know, they'll know about Kay. The Remnants will stay solemn and still as statues, as guards, while Kay and I wait in my room for the old to grow on us.

a history of heart disease

Glen's father dies in a Burger King. Glen is only five and he has to watch his father's big hands fumble at his necktie, then push over paper cups, plastic straws, and finally even people on his way to the floor. Since Glen is only five, he laughs at first because he thinks his father is clowning around with him like he always does. He laughs and laughs until a fat lady in purple stretch pants leans over his father and starts screaming.

When Glen is thirty he is handsome and married, with a little girl and a Golden Retriever named Betsy. He teaches high school kids about rocks and soil. His wife likes to tell him that his head is full of rocks, which is more or less true.

Glen and his wife are having what they refer to as 'marital problems.' She has gained seventy pounds in the last three years. Seventy pounds! Glen cannot understand it. He knows he's an asshole, but Glen hates the way his body sinks into hers, how her new stomach is soft and unformed. It feels like screwing the Pillsbury Doughboy.

Glen was an athlete in school. He was golden and fast, and everyone wanted to be him or be with him. He still runs every morning and now he coaches the high school track team. His wife refers to him as 'Jock,' or sometimes 'The Jock.' He is never sure if this is a compliment or not.

One day after track practice, he is teaching a student named Jenny the right way to wrap a sprain when the phone rings. It is his wife.

Glen, she says, your mother's dead.

When? he says. How?

Just a few hours ago, she tells him, at the Wal-Mart over in Westchester.

Not where, says Glen. *How?*

Oh, sorry—heart attack—she was buying paper towels, I guess. Or at least, that was the only thing in her cart.

Glen is prepared for this. He has been prepared a long time, ever since his father died. He doesn't laugh. He doesn't disbelieve. He sighs and sends Jenny home and picks his daughter up from daycare.

Grandma's heart wasn't very strong, he tells her. It was a good heart, but it wasn't very strong.

His daughter is three and solemn as a poet. She nods, though she doesn't understand. She watches cartoons and always equates good with strong. She doesn't have the capacity to undo metaphors. Glen should really know better, but then Glen has never really been good with children. He's better with dogs. He's better with soil and rocks.

It's probably a good thing, then, that eventually Glen's wife and daughter leave him, after he is caught with Jenny in the teacher's lounge. Glen could blame his idiocy on his fear of getting old, of growing up and dying young. It's what people do in his family. But he doesn't blame anyone except himself. His wife and the judge blame him, too.

Glen gets fired and divorced and charged and convicted. He has to pay a lot of money and spend half the year at a workhouse. Then he goes to live with his brother Peter in San Antonio. He has to leave the Golden Retriever behind, and his small daughter is unwilling to speak to him—at least, that's what his wife says. Ex-wife says.

Peter is married to a woman named Nanette. Nan is right out of a novel, dressed in peasant skirts and stilettos with teased, Texas-sized hair. She smokes long, thin cigarettes and is always rolling her eyes at everything Peter says. But she's pretty and small and Glen lies awake at night and listens to her squealing, Ooh, Peter, ooh, Peter, while the bedposts scrape and thump against the floor.

Peter is a teacher, too. Nan works from home; she makes jewelry and sells it online. Beaded turquoise stuff that Glen's wife would call 'tacky.' He likes the way it lies cool against Nan's warm brown skin, swinging away from her collarbone as she navigates the classifieds and helps Glen try to find a job. It's difficult enough to find work these days, never mind the felony conviction on his record.

Then there's a day when the phone rings; it's the school, for Nan. Peter's had a heart attack. They've taken him to the hospital, and Nan drives Glen there, fast. She is a terrific driver, like an FBI agent in a movie car chase scene.

Glen watches Nan cry into Peter's hospital gown. I told him to drink more wine, the stupid fool, she wails. Red wine is good for the heart, that's what I told him.

At the funeral, people ask where Peter's parents are. Glen tells them he is the only one left. Glen's ex-wife is at the funeral, too, with his daughter. He hugs his daughter tight and sits her on his lap; and although her mother glares at him, she allows the little girl to stay there throughout the service. I wouldn't be here if it wasn't Peter, his ex-wife keeps saying. Peter was a much better person than you.

Nan wears a black lace skirt, like a widow in a Western, and she cries into a handkerchief and everything. Without her, the service would have no dignity at all. The priest speaks in a dry Texan drawl, and Peter's students chew gum and flap their programs and talk in whispers that bounce off the church walls.

His daughter puts her little hand in his sweaty palm. Glen lets it lie there, limp, until Nan reaches over and closes his hand around the child's. She smiles at him around the handkerchief, and smears her mascara with the back of her other hand. Glen feels the warmth of his daughter's hand, like a damp little bird, feels a life ticking and nudging against his own.

all the imaginary people are better at life

Ruby can't stop driving, because if she stops she'll be somewhere. If she's somewhere, she'll be real. All the Ruby atoms in the vicinity will come to a screeching halt in the general shape of her. Then she'll have to deal with all of the issues real people deal with.

No thank you.

So she does another loop around town and ends up sitting in traffic, watching a traffic cop in a florescent green vest wave cars through the intersection. A mosquito flies in and examines the vinyl seats of her car. She smacks it sharply and watches it crumple against her dashboard, shudders at the bright scarlet smear on her palm. She can't stand the sight of small amounts of blood. Big blood, no problem. Buckets of blood, rivers of it, that's okay. But it's the little bits that freak her out, remind her that you bleed and you bleed and you bleed and eventually that will kill you but so slowly you don't even notice until you're dead. Then while you're rotting, you wonder when you could have stopped it, what you could have done to stanch the little bleeding bits. Death by a thousand tiny cuts.

Now, finally in front of her apartment, she has to stop. She hates Home, ever since the boyfriend, Randy, more or less moved himself in. Or not really Home. It's just Here. Just another Here she finds herself in for a while. She parks behind his hideous station wagon and sighs; he must be inside waiting for her. She has explained to him before how much she hates this. It's my apartment, she always says. I need my privacy. He doesn't understand the word my. He eats her privacy like most people eat popcorn.

He is sitting in her favorite chair, the big maroon and gold striped monstrosity left over from her dumpster-diving days. He is sipping Coke through a straw because his dentist told him the soda was rotting his teeth. This makes her crazy, crazy, crazy. He is watching the Home Shopping Network. He is laughing at what the host of the Home Shopping Network program has said. He is the only person she knows who could laugh at the host of a Home Shopping Network program. Take my cubic zirconia, please, she says, and flings her purse onto the couch.

He looks up, smiling and puzzled, his face a fleshy question mark.

Never mind, she says. She touches the couch, the table, the coffee cup left out from last night. She gives these things names in her head: Couch, Table, Cup. They don't seem to fit, the names with the things. She wonders if this is what people mean when they talk about losing your mind. Perhaps bits of her mind are spinning away from her now, the bits containing Couch and Cup and Table and also Boyfriend and Conversation and Paying Attention to What I Am Talking About.

Are you paying attention to what I'm talking about, he asks.

No, she says truthfully. I'm sorry. She is, too. Sorry for him. She sits on the couch next to the chair, her favorite chair. Chair. Talk.

You're thinking of other things, he says.

Yes, she agrees. Yes, probably.

Please, he says. His eyes look shiny, like marbles. Can we just have a normal conversation for once, Ruby? Just talk like people do? We can do that, just talk like people do, right?

Okay, she says, and looks out the window. She knows she's not people but she does not mention this to him. His eyes are too blue; they remind her of Blue Moon ice cream, her least favorite flavor after Bubble Gum.

Are you cheating on me? He blurts it out and stops, looks embarrassed but doesn't take it back.

She doesn't say anything.

Well, he says, are you? Are you seeing anyone else?

She pauses, wishes she could say yes, wishes she could be so cruel.

No, she tells him.

He stands up then, his denim work shirt not quite covering his thin wrists. His wrists are thinner than hers. I don't know what this is, he says. This isn't a relationship, is it?

She decides not to answer. She wouldn't know how to, anyway.

•

Caleb, her imaginary best friend, calls on the space wires from Chicago to complain about the weather. The best part about Caleb is that he has a direct line into her head so she doesn't incur any long distance charges. Ruby has made Caleb an actor, big and blond and very gay, and she loves him more than anyone else in the world. He is not-people and she is not-people. They work well together. He is gay because sex is more exhausting than marathons.

Did you know, he says, did you know that we can't really predict the weather at all? We've polluted the air too much and the greenhouse effect is too far gone or something. We're basically living in a constant state of surprise.

I hate surprises, she says. A few years ago one of her co-workers planned a surprise birthday party for her, and she threw up on the sofa out of shock.

Caleb sighs. I just hate this rain, he says. It makes me feel like somebody wants us quiet down here.

•

Ruby never really had a mom. Her mother was an exotic dancer who ran away right after Ruby was born, leaving nothing behind but three packages of diapers, her wedding ring, and her own name hanging on her daughter's hospital ID bracelet. Ruby Virginia. Ruby hated her name, even though her dad said it meant she was a beautiful jewel. She would have rather been just Jane, plain Jane, like her best friend in elementary school. It seemed like a sensible name, a name that meant nothing and could never make anyone cry.

They say, Ruby, you're like a flame, her father would sing to her. Into my life you came. When he sang that song, she always felt funny; he would look straight at her but his eyes were filled with tears for somebody else. And though I should beware, still I don't care. You thrill me so, I only know, Ruby, it's you.

But it wasn't her at all. She knew that. It made her sad with someone else's grief.

•

Ruby buys a latte and a newspaper. She finds a table, sips her drink, and circles things that have nothing to do with her. She is a compulsive list-maker, note-taker, and circler. She buys computer magazines and circles models she likes, peruses classifieds and circles garage sales she doesn't intend to go to, used cars she doesn't want to buy. Now she circles an ad for heartworm medication. There is a worm in my heart, she thinks.

He doesn't move from that chair anymore, says the woman at the next table over. Yep, he just sits there and rocks back and forth, watches CNN sometimes.

I know, I know, it's depressing, says the woman's companion. Two women sipping iced coffees and discussing their...father?

Grandfather? Brother? It is easy enough to overhear their conversation. They speak with the long, rounded vowels of the upper Midwest, too loudly and with an abandon that embarrasses Ruby. Some people suck so badly at being alive, she thinks.

One of the women, the younger one, has frizzy dark blonde hair tucked behind her ears and wears an oversized T-shirt with sweat stains under the armpits. She shakes her head, sending frizz flying in every direction, and says, he's just completely sedimentary now. The other woman nods in agreement, and Ruby snorts. She pictures the man in question slowly calcifying, bits of rock building up on this arm, or that toe. His chest soon looks like the Rockies without the climbers and so he goes to see his doctor.

Doc, he asks, Doc, what's wrong with me?

Not to worry, Ted (or Bill or Fred or George or Bob), you're just sedimentary. No big deal. Just watch out for the tectonics; they might give you a little heartburn.

Ruby laughs and laughs at her scenario, knocking over her latte, and the two women turn and stare along with half the cafe. She sobers then. She has drawn far too much attention to herself. They will see she isn't like them. She feels her arms, suddenly colder. It's not a worm at all, she thinks. Her heart is slowly turning to stone. Even now, it seems, her heart is calcifying at so rapid a rate that soon there will be nothing left but a strange, slightly pliable boulder.

•

Sometimes she wonders if Randy is using her for her apartment. Somehow all of his things are migrating there, like strange species in the process of relocation. A nail clippers here, a couple of shirts there, until her place became more full of him than her. She wonders sometimes if she properly exists anymore, or if through some unconscious philanthropic gesture she's given too much of her space to Randy to occupy it herself.

When Randy gets ready in the morning he tries too hard to be quiet and it always wakes her. She can hear his 'quiet' walk, slow and stretched and out of time like an astronaut on the moon. His huge feet scrape the carpet and she always sighs loudly, flings the pillow over her head, sometimes groans for extra effect. Sorry, he'll whisper. Sorry, Beautiful, didn't mean to wake you. She hates that he whispers even though she's awake and there's no one else in the house, hates that he is always sorry, hates that he calls her Beautiful, hates that he says the same things over and over until her nerves vibrate and snap like guitar strings. When they do it he thinks she's crying because she loves him. He licks her tears and calls her Ruby, baby, and she thinks about how the back of his head would look blown off by a shotgun.

This morning she waits until she hears his car pull out, then calls in sick to work. This is the fifth time in two weeks, and she thinks she may be fired soon. Caleb calls and she turns up the frequency in her head to listen. Are you okay? he asks. He sounds truly concerned, and she is touched.

When you and Lorenzo are doing it, she asks, does he call you Beautiful? Lorenzo is Caleb's imaginary boyfriend. He is dark and tall and excitable, and he kisses Ruby's cheeks when they see one another. He smells like Europe.

What? No, he doesn't say much of anything, Caleb says down the wires. Ruby, what's wrong with you? Why aren't you at work?

You and I can't pretend to do the things people do, she says. We don't need to go to work. We don't need to provide for our families.

Look, Caleb says. I'm imaginary but you're a real person. Jesus, Ruby. You have to eat real food. You have to pay real rent. You're not imaginary, dude. You're just crazy, that's all. You just really suck at being alive.

Fuck you, she tells him. She hangs up her imaginary phone. But angry as she is, she envies Caleb. He seems so much more put together than she is. Probably because he only has to get his shit together within the small spaces she's created for him. But still. He's better at life; that's for sure.

•

When she was five, Ruby's father built her a child-sized house of cards, just big enough for her to play in. The sides were cardboard boxes painted to look like playing cards; a jack, a king, a queen, and an ace on four walls. All hearts.

She would take her book in there and sit for hours, tucked away in a house inside a basement inside a house. She thinks now that she has always been a person that needs layers. Not a scarf or a sweater, but walls between her and other people. A series of homes within homes. A series of places to hide.

•

She decides to spend the day at the bookstore. She heads for the section marked 'Travel' and finds a hardbound road atlas. She sits on the floor and balances it in her lap, her hair brushing over a corn-colored Iowa. She watches the smallish balding man leafing restlessly through a copy of The Really Unofficial Guide to Disney World, and she drops down, lightly, into the land of Other People. She tilts her head, regards him with curiosity.

What's your favorite state? she asks.

He turns to her and frowns a little, and she begins to feel disappointed. She is just starting to think that he is too much like her, too dependent on layers, too much in love with his Personal Space, when he smiles a little and says, Maine, I think.

Really, Maine? Why? She knows nothing about Maine.

We used to go to my grandparents' cottage up there when I was a kid, he says. It's really beautiful. He shakes his head, and with embarrassment she sees that his shirt is unbuttoned too much, reveals too large a patch of flabby white chest, maggoty-looking and hairless. She looks down at her book, flips the pages until she finds the map of Maine. The man leans down and stabs his stubby finger down on a dot near the coast. Great Pond, he says. That's where the cottage was. He smiles again and she begins to worry a little. She thinks he can probably see down her shirt. She shifts a little and her long hair falls into her eyes, and when she brushes it back she is sure he takes this for flirting. Then she notices a ring on his left ring finger and relaxes a little.

So what happened to it?

Maine? It's still there, I hope, he says.

No, your grandparents' cottage. She tries to smile encouragingly, finds it a foreign sensation. It's like her muscles have forgotten the trick of it. Do you still go there? she asks.

His face changes. She's asked the wrong question. She is always asking the wrong questions. He straightens and picks up his book, starts to walk out of the aisle. It's gone now, he says, mostly to himself. And she wishes she could feel bad, but all she really feels is relief because she doesn't have to look at his maggoty chest anymore. She thrusts her face into the atlas and pretends to be absolutely engrossed in Maine's highway system.

And then she is engrossed. Not by the highway system, but by the idea of Maine as somewhere she could go. She would like to drive to Maine, maybe live in a cottage on the ocean and catch lobster and never see any people at all unless she goes down to talk with the local fishermen or something. She could get a dog and walk it. Yes. Ruby can picture herself in deepest July, wearing floral print dresses and walking everywhere, everywhere barefoot and sea-salted and hardened as hardtack. Yes. It sounds right. It sounds like a place to be. A refuge.

She lugs the big book to the checkout counter and drops it in front of the cashier, a woman in a terrifying sweater. It's one of those boutique-y things, probably handmade, with what may or may not be a cluster of grapes embroidered in bright purple thread on fake denim. It looks like it's winking at her. She tries hard not to be distracted by the sweater, but it's difficult, when one does not fully exist, to concentrate on much of anything.

I'm going to Maine, Ruby tells the woman and her sweater.

Neither the woman nor the sweater responds.

I'm going to live there, Ruby says, in a cottage by the sea.

Mmm, says the clerk. That'll be $39.99, please.

Ruby hands her a fifty. I'm finally having a nervous breakdown, she says. I think this must be part of it. I've been expecting it for so long, it's almost a relief.

The woman nods and gives her the change. She tosses the receipt into the bag and hands it to Ruby.

Ruby turns to go, but then stops and turns back. She feels she should say something else, something really meaningful and lasting. A farewell of sorts. But as usual, she can't think of anything. The sweater, too, remains silent in its own jovial, winking way. She feels a kinship with it.

•

Ruby calls Caleb on the space wires when she stops at the gas station. What are you talking about, Maine? he asks. Or rather, she has him ask.

I'm going there. To Maine. Right now, she tells him.

For how long?

Indefinitely, she says. She can tell he doesn't believe her, but because he loves her he will humor her slightly. And also because he is a figment of her imagination.

And what, exactly, he asks, do you plan to do in Maine with no money, no job, and no place to stay?

How do you know I don't have any money? Anyway, I don't need any money, she says. I'm going to run around barefoot and catch lobsters for food and wear Liberty print dresses and make all the local fishermen fall in love with me.

A long sigh from Caleb rustles down the wires. Ruby, he says. He sounds very serious. People don't actually do those things.

She is quiet, says nothing. The speaker wires fizzle and fade out. Even her imaginary person is exasperated with her now.

Ruby knows she is selfish and silent and stark-raving. This is why she has to go away from everyone. This is why she has to go away from Randy, plus all of the other reasons that she can't be with him. For starters, he will want to marry her, and then they will officially be Randy and Ruby Richter. They will have to start wearing matching track suits with puffy designs sewn on them. They will have to start watching sporting events, and eating chips 'n dip, and they will have to say it just like that: chips 'n dip. Eventually they will have children, and they will have to give them names that start with R, like Ruthanne and Remus and Roxy and of course, Randy, Jr. They will acquire a minivan. They will use the minivan to shuttle children back and forth to soccer and baseball games, to carry loud and terrible musical instruments to band practice. Ruby will go slowly mad until they have to put her in a padded cell shaped like a kitchen, because all she will want to do is bake brownies and cookies and cakes with R names painted on in frosting, blue for the boys and pink for the girls and yellow for the ones who haven't yet decided what they want to be, beautiful or strong because in this world you can't be both.

She stands with her cell phone in her hand, debating whether or not to call him. She decides to text him instead, hoping he'll be too busy at work to check his phone. Then she goes inside to pay for the gas. She flirts a bit with the young guy at the counter, a flame-haired and freckled type she'd never seriously consider. She feels so good, in fact, that she gives him her last five as a tip and purchases some wrap-around Oakleys with her credit card. With the sunglasses firmly wrapped-around her head, she strolls out the door.

What a piece of work is a man, she says grandly, loudly. People turn and stare. At first she smiles at them all, but then she gets depressed because the only Shakespeare she knows by heart is the same Shakespeare everybody else knows by heart. Then she gets even more depressed, because the only opportunity she has to quote Shakespeare is to a bunch of people pumping gas who are also trying to avoid making eye contact with her.

A couple of teenaged boys in a beat-up blue Honda pull up to the curb, their music forced so hard through crappy speakers it squeals and cracks against distorted beats. A kid in the white baseball cap is stepping out of the passenger side. Go fuck your mom, he says to the kid driving the car. They both suddenly giggle and Ruby turns to see what they're giggling at and it's Randy—oh, god—standing in the rain and sniffling.

He's wearing his stupid Broncos sweatshirt that's about ten sizes too small and leaves his hairy skinny wrists exposed. He looks as if he can't decide whether to smile. He looks constipated. How is he here? Is he really here? Or has she begun to conjure even the people she loathes, her imagination so broken it can no longer do anything helpful?

What a piece of work is a man, she repeats, and fingers the keys in her jacket pocket. It has begun storming in earnest. The sky has turned a purplish-blue color, People are running for their cars now, and diving under the awnings, but Randy doesn't move. He just stands there, water washing his features away and turning his face red and mushy-looking. Ruby thinks she could run past him to her car. Maybe she could distract him somehow? Throw something one way, then run quickly in the other direction?

I love you, he says, and she thinks she could stab him with her keys. She could say he was an attacker. No one would know. There is nothing to link him to her: no bills with both their names, no apartment lease, nothing. There is nothing permanent about their relationship, nothing that's left to last.

Well, he yells, over the thunder. Her jeans are already so soaked they tug and threaten to fall right off. She feels distracted by this, distracted by everything. She pictures herself in judgment, standing before God or whoever, shrugging when asked, Why didn't you accomplish anything in your time on Earth?

I just got distracted, she imagines herself saying. She knows, of course, that she is full of shit, full of excuses. Everything that's ever happened to her has been an excuse to retreat into her worst personality. To close herself off and build a new exterior; an endless set of matryoshka dolls wearing her face and saying nothing.

I'm sorry, she says, because really there's never anything else to say about life. Then she slips sideways past Randy and gets into her car. She shuts the door and watches as the wind blows rain around his outline, smudges and then blots it out.

the city outside of itself

The City longed to travel. He hadn't been anywhere in ages, and wanted to see what things looked liked outside of himself. So the City asked his best friend Tammie if she would mind giving him a lift. Tammie took her gum out of her mouth and twirled it around and around her index finger, pink on peach on pink, while she thought about it.

Okay, she said, popping the gum back into her mouth. The City thought that was kind of gross, but he didn't say anything since she had agreed to give him a lift. He barely had time to wince before Tammie was hoisting him up onto her shoulders, where he rested like the set of a complicated play.

Where are we going? Tammie asked. The City hadn't thought this part through. He asked Tammie to give him some time, so she tried on dresses at Topshop while the City read through his guidebooks. Hurry up, she said through a layer of fuchsia organza. I'm just about done here. While she was ringing up her stuff, the City decided on Mexico. Airfare was dirt cheap. Plus he'd never been there before, even though it wasn't that far away. He could get back pretty quickly if he needed to.

Tammie thanked the clerk and took her bag. The City was super excited; he was scribbling notes about all the places they would go, like the ruins, and the beaches, and then maybe to visit his cousin, Mexico City. That would be sweet. The City told Tammie he'd decided, but she shook her head.

I changed my mind, she said. You're getting really heavy, and anyway, I have to go to work tomorrow. And she lifted the City from her shoulders and settled him gently back into the spot where he belonged, the spot that he'd worn into the general shape of him from all the years of being there.

The streets of the City were flooded with sadness for a long while after that.

the ghosts eat more air

There are no clocks in the land of the dead. There are no wristwatches, no calendars, no way to keep track of time. The spirits do not make appointments; they will get around to everything eventually. The dead need not keep time. Time keeps them. They are prisoners trapped in it as surely as flies in honey, and nothing really moves, nothing changes—though everything slowly, gradually shifts, oozes, evolves, dries up, blows away. The dead are as dead as doornails. Their world is a flat place of pooling ink and vapor, of streets stacked one over another, since no one minds sharing space after life.

As a consequence of all this stacking, the land of the dead is no bigger than a small cottage. And since it is so small, and since nothing ever really happens there, when something momentous finally occurs the dead are instantly stirred. Souls dry as dust and dormant for centuries flip over in their beds and groan a little. Newer souls, still shaky and vibrant as wet paint, flutter about like moths and chatter to one another.

Here is what happens: a living child is born. No one can say how it happens; in the long memories of the dead it has certainly never happened before. The news drifts like fog through the land of the dead until every single spirit is soaked through, shivering in their almost-bodies, afraid of what this birth might portend. The seriousness of the situation propels the dead into hushed, halting conversation. A vote of sorts is taken. The child, it is decided, will be cast out to dwell with the living, where she can be cared for. But her kin will not abandon her completely. She will be followed, watched over; all her life she will be divided, with her feet in the Styx and her head in the stars.

•

It's the opposite of being with people, which is maybe why the father likes it so much. The arms of the ghosts swirl twirl round him like spaghetti, brush past his face, comfort him without grabbing, holding, pushing, or pulling. Without the sweat and sour rot all people seem to leak. Death erases that. The ghosts smell like nothing, feel like breezes, whisper on their way to wherever they're bound. There is no regret in them. They separate him from humans, help him observe and inquire. They help him understand how small people are.

He has forbidden TV, forbidden radio, forbidden wireless of any kind in his home. The signals would interfere with those the ghosts give off, with the live trails they leave looping through the air. His daughter begs for TV, for an email account or a cell phone, and traipses over to the neighbor kids' houses on weeknights to watch her shows and surf the web. She tells the neighbor kids her father is crazy. She rolls her eyes and tells the neighbor kids that the ghosts are more important than she is. It has been this way since she was very small. Since her mother died, really. Before that, the ghosts were more like mice. After that, they invaded, rolling through the plaster and carpet and wood-paneling like waves of black mold.

Her father says he draws inspiration from the ghosts. He says it is important to be good at what you do, and living with the dead has made him very good. But the daughter hates the dead. They scare her more now than when she was a child. She didn't notice, before, how they keep on saying the same things, over and over in breathless buzzes. She didn't notice how they cling to her like lichen to a rock, how they smile in the dark when they think no one is watching, how they have no faces but smile in the dark just the same. She notices now and has begun to feel afraid.

•

The father is an actor and the mother is dead. These are the two most important facts in the daughter's life. Third most important: the ghosts themselves, the fact of them, the presence they create in nearly every space she occupies. They cluster around her sometimes in a way that is just shy of alarming. But they seem mostly to stick to the house. They seem to love her father most.

She doesn't look for her mother in the herd of the dead. That is not the point of the ghosts. No one would recognize these creatures as anything like people; they are so far removed from the world that they have no memory of who they were. She is not sure they were ever human at all. All she knows is that they are as dead as death can make you.

Still, their milky eyes follow her everywhere, faintly curious, a dull kind of play still lit within them. She swears they sprinkle little secrets where she walks, like sugar in her path. She doesn't want their secrets. She wouldn't want anything the dead could give her, unless it is her mother back again.

Before she got sick, her mother had been strong and hard as bullets. She was the one who got things done. Her father had always been less present, even before the ghosts. Onstage, he took up so much space—the expansive, entitled space of a king—but at home he did the dishes slowly, humming old songs out of tune until he seemed more like background than family. When she was small, the daughter thought everyone's life was like this. Your mother was the center of everything, the sun; your father was the faraway planet who opened into something wonderful only under the lights, while you sat in the dark, a spectator, and listened to words that only sounded like the words you knew. The ghosts were your soft and small friends, almost imaginary, skittering through the walls and along the ceiling. Clustering round your soul at night for warmth.

Then the ghosts changed. It is her father's fault that they changed. It was after her mother died that her father's heart caved in on itself, became a vast black hole. And the ghosts began drifting in.

•

Her father thinks the dead help him understand what people are really like, from all directions and angles, inside out and close up. He thinks the dead elevate his art. His daughter thinks she would like to place hundreds of TVs, cell phones, wireless cards, radios and laptops all over their house, until the shapes of the ghosts are burned clean away in the electromagnetic chorus. I need to be online to do this project, she tells her father. Can we please get wireless?

Go over to the Jacobsons', her father says, frowning over his Rice Krispies. He has just learned he has been cast as Polonius instead of Hamlet. He is furious; he is a little old, yes, but he and the ghosts have been discussing the unknown country and he felt prepared to play Hamlet. His heart hurts as Hamlet's did. He hangs at the edge of the world like Hamlet did. He knows the ghosts are inarticulate, and mostly silent, but they are the only returning travelers he knows and so he must make do.

Mrs. Jacobson says I can't always use their computer, his daughter tells him. She says you really ought to buy me one.

Her father says nothing. He chews and thinks Hamlet-shaped thoughts.

Mrs. Jacobson, announces his daughter, says a man paralyzed

by grief is one thing, but a man paralyzed by grief for seven years is another thing entirely.

The father looks up from his Krispies, a scowl stretched across his face. Who the hell is she to say something like that? Just who the hell is she?

His daughter shrugs. Okay, I'll stay late tonight at the library, she says. I'll use the computers there. *And the ghosts won't be able to distract me*, she thinks. *They won't be able to make me feel cold and strange.*

She suspects the ghosts came tumbling in, faster and faster, more and more of them, because of her mother's death. Because, really, of her and her father. They make strong graves for these ghosts. Their house is a bed of quiet sadness. She sighs to think of it, feels the ghosts wash blue and cold through her chest and head at the thought. She shivers. When she was small, just after her mother died, the ghosts were tender with her when her father was not. They kept her safe. They absorbed her tears in their whispers and kept certain things from her, things that children might be afraid to know. Mysteries were hidden; the darkest secrets of the buried stayed behind with their bodies while their spirits went wandering. Her father could see the ghosts' thoughts drift like smoke above his daughter's head, smudging past her ears and eyes and mouth, but never entering. This is how the ghosts are with children.

With adults, it is different. The ghosts know how much they can do, and they keep their distance until the children are no longer children. Then they begin to enter, to play, to unburden themselves of their soft, faded stories, grown strange and scallop-edged like someone has been at them with pinking shears. They begin to blow into the nostrils, the eye sockets, float down the throat and into every hole they can find in the body. They look for a temporary home, for a memory drought, for an empty shell to feel whole in for a little while. They stroke and scrape and they know nothing of what they are supposed to be, for they have no clear thoughts and only a vague, confusing notion of how sensations are supposed to feel. They move hands down, move bodies up to meet them, blow hot breaths on eyelids and teeth and spill imaginary liquids down the pages of books and the legs of tables. They are careless with human flesh.

•

Could there be such a thing as ghosts, the daughter asks her Biology teacher. Mr. Phipps smiles, and some of the boys snort with laughter. No, really, she says. It's important. I need to know. Scientifically, I mean, could there be such a thing?

Of course not, says Mr. Phipps. You kids tell too many ghost stories, watch too many slasher movies. You scare yourselves silly. He turns back to the white board, labels a picture of a liver. L-I-V-E-R. We are deathers, the daughter thinks. We are the opposite of livers. A note sails through the air, lands on the daughter's desk. She unfolds it, reads the letters inked in blue: Q: COULD THERE BE SUCH A THING AS RETARDS? SCIENTIFICALLY, I MEAN? Her name is the answer.

She folds the note back into a square, then a smaller square, then a smaller one, until the paper won't bend anymore. She flicks it onto the ground and watches it lie there, small and white and poisonous, choking her from the floor. Lately she feels like she is always choking, always trying to find more air. She is so apart, a wall of water away, drowning in a world that no one else can see.

•

The vice-principal frowns. You're telling me your father is some kind of ghost hunter, or something?

No, no, says the daughter. He feeds the ghosts. We feed them. He says they need us.

The vice-principal sighs, pushes back her chair, and stands up. I know how difficult it can be, she starts, to lose a loved one. I—

I'm not making it up, says the daughter. It's not about my mother, and I'm not making it up. She folds her arms. Stares at the vice-principal with light blue eyes like ice crystals. They make the vice-principal uncomfortable. They seem unlikely to melt. They seem diamond hard. Maybe she can see ghosts, the vice-principal thinks. She certainly is the strangest girl the vice-principal has ever met. You'd never believe she could go to prom, or play soccer, or kiss a boy, or even cheat on a test. She seems like a little dead thing, not quite of this world.

The girl appears to be a mind reader also, because she suddenly responds to what the vice-principal has not said aloud. I'm not strange, she says. I don't want the ghosts. It's my father who's done this to both of us. Go talk to him, not me. He's the one.

For some reason, the vice-principal shivers at this. For some reason, it feels like this might be true.

•

The father tried to love a person again, once. The girlfriend was an actress, kind but high-strung and sensitive. She never noticed the ghosts. She moved in a week before the daughter's tenth birthday, and moved out exactly two years later. The daughter actually circled the date on their Skyscrapers of the World calendar. The ghosts were celebrating, zipping about like faint fireworks, so she tried to make it seem like a celebration, too. But really, she was sad. She had liked the girlfriend. The girlfriend remembered things like holidays and school supplies. She had sunny blonde hair, and she would let the daughter play with her makeup sometimes, and when she was there the house seemed a little more like a home again. A place where *people* lived.

There was an awful row one day, and then the next day the girlfriend was standing at the top of the stairs with her silver suitcases packed, one in each hand. Right before she left forever, she put her hand on the daughter's shoulder and told her to be good. And leave this house, she said. As soon as you can, leave it like I'm leaving it. Take everything you own and don't ever come back.

Get out, said the father. Get out of my house. The girlfriend bit her lip and the daughter could see she had been crying hard, black smudges under her eyes and her pretty lips all swollen and red. The ghosts were practically pushing her out of the house, and she went stumbling out the door and into a taxi waiting in the driveway. And that was the last they ever saw of the girlfriend. Yellow hair and silver suitcases, disappearing into a green cab.

Good riddance, said the father. The ghosts flung themselves across his shoulders in agreement. After that, they always lived alone, the daughter and the father, wrapped in their ghosts and their loneliness.

•

The daughter wakes up screaming. She looks across the room and sees in her mirror a gaping violet-black void, and ghosts streaming out, spinning free of it like fast winds off the desert. One of them flies too fast, and his skidding stop over her leaves a long narrow burn mark on her arm.

Don't be afraid, her father says when he comes to check on her. The ghosts like to be close to us. They feed off of our warmth. They *need* us.

His daughter shivers under the blankets and covers her head with her pillow. No one else has ghosts, her muffled voice says. No one else even believes in them. She massages her hurt arm.

That's why we are very, very lucky, says her father. She can't see him but she can tell his smile is pointed, rat-like; she hates him just now.

Yes, she says weakly, knowing how useless it is to argue. Her father is in love with the ghosts. She knows this now. This is why there have been no more girlfriends. He is farther away than ever. He is becoming like them, less often troubled but more volatile when shaken, waiting for something, always waiting. The ghosts have an eternity to wait, of course, while she does not. Their patience seduces her father, astounds him, turns the short line of life into a long horizon bending somewhere dim and hopeful. He likes the idea of waiting forever, with calm care and just a hint of being. Sometimes the daughter wonders if she actually died with her mother; if she is the real ghost after all. She is so clearly the intruder in her home.

•

The daughter gets the idea from a documentary about Thomas Edison. It shows how he electrocuted an elephant in the zoo to make sure his alternating current could kill something big. The zoo staff had to use a ship's hawser to restrain the elephant, whose name was Topsy. Her last meal was a sack of carrots laced with cyanide, just in case. They put wooden shoes on her feet, fixed with copper electrodes. Edison's people ran a wire cable from Topsy's new clogs straight to Edison's plant. When Edison gave the signal his technicians threw the switch and poured a 6,600 volt charge of alternating current into Topsy's huge frame. She died instantly and fell over sideways, kicking up so much dust as she hit the ground that she disappeared for a moment behind it.

The daughter stares at the documentary film of Topsy's dust-covered bulk, splayed out and still twitching slightly, smoke curling up from around her feet. The ghosts hate electricity. The daughter wonders how she would restrain the ghosts like Edison restrained the elephant. Could she use some sort of wireless signal to keep them in? Surround the house with cell phones somehow? She thinks she could destroy them with electricity, by touching wires to wires. That part is easy enough. The hard part would be keeping them there long enough to destroy them. Ghosts are more dangerous than a mad elephant.

Then, suddenly, she has it. A brilliant idea. She only has to call the television satellite company and sound adult enough. Apparently, she succeeds, because here is the white truck now, pulling up outside, and there is the ladder the workmen will climb to the roof to install the new dish. The ghosts are agitated, more solid than she has ever seen them. Even the workmen seem to notice. Windy out today, says one, as another looks around bewildered.

Doesn't look windy, he says.

Yeah, says the first guy, but I can feel it. I can barely keep hold of my tools.

The ghosts know it is the daughter's doing. They know. They break off their attack, seep into her bedroom through the walls, and swirl and swirl around her, faster and faster, until she starts to rise into the air. No! she says. Stop it! Put me down! The ghosts have never been able to lift her before. This is scary. This is serious.

Then the door slams and her father is there; he is furious and not at the ghosts, but then he sees her through the swarm of spirits holding her under the roof and he shouts, he sweeps them away, he catches her as she falls and sets her down gently on her own bed. He puts his face in his huge hands and starts to cry, something the daughter has never seen him do for real. He does it a different way on the stage. She watches with interest until he lifts his red-rimmed eyes to hers, says softly, you can't chase out the ghosts. They came with you. They're yours.

No, says the daughter. That's not true. They're your ghosts. I don't want them.

You may not want them, says the father, but they're yours just the same. They gave you to us. They brought you to us, your mom and me. And they stayed, to watch over you, I guess.

Outside the satellite company workers are loading the dish back into their van. The daughter watches them and knows she has lost. She knows she can't kill the ghosts. Especially not now that she knows they belong to her. That doesn't mean, though, that she has given up on ridding herself of them. She doesn't care that they came with her. She has got to leave them behind, all of them, or they will soon swallow her up.

•

It is fourteen years ago. A man and a woman walk into a funeral. It sounds like a joke, but it is not a joke. A man and a woman walk into a funeral and before the funeral baked meats have a chance to cool, they've fallen dreadfully and stupidly in love and it is not a joke. Not with each other—they are already in love with each other—but with the baby they find, wrapped in thin cotton sheets and stowed away in the church coat closet. Should we take her? asks the woman, brushing her fingertips above the baby's odd, light blue eyes, over the translucent lids and lashes.

We should shelter her, says the man, and he smiles at the baby, who is batting at something neither of the adults can see.

Isn't she feisty? asks the mother, watching as the daughter shadowboxes away. The mother never could see the ghosts. The mother could never save her daughter, though she kept trying until the day she died.

•

When the world finally comes to save her, her father is away at rehearsal. The daughter waits with two women in the kitchen, makes them coffee and offers them Oreos. She is so excited she forgets to eat hers. She can feel the ghosts pushing angrily at the strangers, pulling at their clothing, blowing forgetting thoughts into their faces. The women blink and wave the dead away like gnats.

When her father walks in, he does his best imitation of a real father, but it is no good. The women can see he is acting. They talk to him in the living room for a long, long time. The daughter hears her father yelling. She can feel him upsetting the ghosts, their spirits growing thin and syrupy. They slink around her, ghost-blobs with question marks for faces, but she has no answers to give them. When they finally return to the kitchen, the women clear their throats and ask her if she believes there are ghosts in her home.

The daughter's eyes drop, and she cannot look at her father. She can hear him starting to cry, but she can also hear the ghosts applauding faintly and she knows this is just more acting; the way he cries on stage. No, of course not, she says, and the screams of the dead are high and heavy. The air goes grey. One of the women nods and tells the daughter to pack her things, that she's going to live somewhere else for a while. As she follows the women up the stairs, her father watches with a ghost at either shoulder; the ghosts smile with their almost-faces. He feels the terrible loss gathering in his throat, but the ghosts whisper to him, sing to him of how much room she took up, how much air the ghosts need after all. She is too much people now; she is no longer one of their own. She has to go.

He swallows the loss down hard, feels faint, and pretends to admire this new hazy view of the hallway, his vision ringed with black. *There is nothing permanent here anyway*, he thinks. *There is nothing on Earth we should treasure*. The silence after the door shuts is the mammoth silence between the cradle and the grave.

when other people's lives fall into your lap

They practically fall out of bed when the dude starts yelling outside. He's got a loud yell, a dangerous, scary yell, worse than angry because you can tell his rage is slipping into the space outside the brain where it pools and pushes against the skull and makes you do things, Things, THINGS.

It's just one of the homeless guys trying to get in, she says. She moves closer to him, and they lie very still in the bed hoping someone has properly shut the back door.

But no, someone hasn't, and they hear a flat bang, and the door swings open, and suddenly a woman is screaming in the laundry room next door, high and horrible and help me, help me, she's actually saying that, shrieking it, and they hear a large something slamming against the dryers over and over. The noise is shocking, gruesome. Meat hitting metal. The yeller's voice is muffled, he's all messed up, he's mumbling now but the rage is spilling over worse than ever. I'll kill you motherfucker, I'll kill you, he keeps saying, and the screaming and slamming won't stop.

Until it does, suddenly. And everything goes quieter than space.

They call the cops in a whisper and sit huddled in front of the door in the dark, shushing each other. She wishes they had a gun in the apartment; she could have run to the laundry room and shot him, maybe not in the head but in the chest or leg, somewhere meaty. Somewhere substantial. She's heard that if you're high on PCP or whatever you don't feel pain and you don't die right away, that your momentum keeps you moving forward, all the bone and blood and muscle in you hanging together until the adrenaline rush finally goes for good.

Oh my god, she says. Oh my god, it's just like Kitty Genovese. How could we not have saved her? She puts her palms flat against the floor, presses hard to feel the wood fibers digging into her skin. I think that woman's dead, she says. Don't you think she's dead?

Shhhhhh, he says, we don't know. We don't know anything. His chin rests on his knees; his arms are wrapped tight around his legs. They shiver in their underwear. They hear sirens: close, closer, here they are now in the back parking lot. Lights flash outside, soft and red through the blinds.

She starts to cry. How will we live like people now, she says. How will we. It's not a question, even though it sounds like one.

if you don't believe,
they go away

The little girl is strange, and special, and full of stories; the man across the hall is tall, and old, and lonely. He has no one to talk to but the little girl. Every day the man comes home from work and jingles his keys in front of his door, and like a cat the little girl bursts out of the apartment across the hall and flings herself at him. And she follows him into his apartment and he makes her cocoa, and she sits at his tiny kitchen table and takes little sips, wiping the foam from her lips in between. And she tells him stories.

Like the one about how in France there was a monster with a giant claw for a hand, and he was five thousand feet tall, and he could have ripped down the Eiffel Tower and killed all the people with his poisonous breath if he wanted to. But he didn't want to. He was a kind and gentle monster, and he couldn't help that he had a claw for a hand and poisonous breath, so he just lived mostly in the sea and ate fish. And since he could have killed them all but didn't, the people worshipped him (from a safe distance) and he was happy.

The little girl is my sister, and we are waiting for her to come home so we can eat dinner. She has always been full of stories. Even when she was just learning to talk, she told us her peas were really bullets, and if she ate them her mouth would turn into a silver gun and she would shoot us all, bam, bam, bam. She told Miss Shirley at KinderCare that all the dogs in the world had a terrible disease, and soon they would turn purple and start shrinking, smaller and smaller, until they were tiny enough that all the cats would swallow them like mice. Miss Shirley called my mother and said, Your daughter has emotional problems.

No, no, my mother told Miss Shirley, my daughter just has stories. Like stories was a condition. Which I guess maybe it is.

So my mother smiles when my sister tells us tales about the man across the hall. She tells us how the man sometimes turns into a small white dog, or sometimes into a snake. And that one time he turned her into a snake, too, and showed her how to slither under the doors and furniture without any feet or hands. She says that he has a magical garden, right under the windowsill, with hundreds of different kinds of exotic flowers. But if you don't believe, she says, they go away.

My sister puts on her yellow rain boots before school every morning, even when the sun is shining. She calls them her Good Boots. They are magical, she says, and when she walks they glow like a thousand fireflies and keep away all enemies and evil things. The kids at school make fun of her. They think my family must be poor, that she doesn't have any other shoes to wear. I tell them my sister is crazy.

Are you visiting that man across the hall again today? my mother asks. My sister rolls her eyes and says yes, of course, she visits the man every day. Duh. She tells us how the man has said that soon, he will teach her how to turn into a robin, and they will fly south for the winter and return in the spring. She will be sad to miss the winter. She likes stomping in the snow in the Good Boots, she says, but instead she will make friends with colorful birds and fall asleep listening to jungle noises and tropical rain.

My dad pours cream into his coffee and shakes his head. I don't know where you get your imagination, he says, but it certainly isn't from the rest of us.

It's true. We have no stories to tell, my mother and dad and me.

We are flat, two-dimensional; stories do not burst from our heads like roses. We have no real character arc. We go from home to school to soccer practice to work and back and we never change. And we don't believe in magic glowing boots, or little girls who turn into birds and snakes and silver guns.

One day we wait for my sister to come home from dinner, just like we do every night. Only this time we wait, and wait, and wait, until finally my dad gets angry and goes across the hall and bangs on the door. There is no answer. When the police finally arrive and force open the door, my mother grabs at my father's shirt in panic. There is nothing at all in the apartment: no tall old man, no little girl, no furniture, no rugs or plates or knives or cups of cocoa. There is nothing at all in the dim, dingy place except for a pair of yellow rain boots, neatly placed under the living room windowsill.

My little sister is full of stories, but she has packed them up and flown. We eat our dinners in silence and at night our dreams are blank and empty. We watch the snows fall and melt and fall again, and we dare not make up stories of our own. None of us will admit it, but we are a restless audience; we are waiting and watching for the first signs of spring.

feral children:
a collective history

They are raised by wolves or they are raised by apes or they are raised by gazelle or donkeys or dolphins, by dogs or goats or cats or birds or bears or even bees. They suckle at teats when tiny, but later they chew grass, lettuce, kelp, slurp pollen and search for the softest, sweetest apples littering the ground., Or else learn to tear open carcasses with tiny baby teeth, to catch small fish with pudgy hands, to stalk prey on silent wobbly baby legs, baby noses sniffing out the tangy copper trail of blood.

Before they can learn wild ways, there must be a parting from the human parents. The children are cast out of the home, the village, the castle, shack, orphanage, hospital, shtetl. Or they are stolen from the crib. They are abandoned, unwanted, left in the woods to die. They run away. They are given to the pack, the animal mothers, to the Earth, as a ritual sacrifice or in accordance with Fate or to hide the child from murderous uncle, stepmother, father, or king.

They inhabit the woods of Croatia, Romania, Denmark, Austria, Canada, Siberia, the Ukraine, Poland, Argentina, Germany. Or the wilds of Brazil, Uganda, South Africa, Sierra Leone, Kenya, Indonesia, Burundi, Mauritania. Or the waters of the Aegean Sea, the Black Sea, the Indian Ocean, the coast of the Pacific Northwest. Or the property-lining bushes of suburban tract housing, vast garbage dumps, hollow logs, even wide, flat rocks and the soft soil after a hard rain.

After death they can sometimes be found in constellations,

scattered over the surface of the sky like seed pearls.

They speak no language at first. They are grunters, groaners, squealers, squawkers; guttural sounds grow up through their vocal cords, wild and tangled and green. They do not sound like their animal brothers and sisters. They try but cannot quite replicate the sounds the muzzle or the wings or the long nose and narrow jaw produce. There is a buzz in the ear, a slight imbalance, a tremor in the tongue with each attempt. Their animal speech is accented, a reminder that these children will not stay wild forever. Not wild and free like wind, like biting like galloping and snorting and swimming and nuzzling and guzzling and piling up together in good raw wet fur smells forever.

Never forever. There comes a point, always, where the wolf-child or the goat-child or the bear-child or the monkey-child is discovered by humans. There is power in this inverse of the usual myth: A child is found, is a foundling, will be founder of the new civilization or dynasty or world. There is power in the second beginning, the tumbling out from the wild woods' womb, the original loss glossed over and made to disappear.

And so the child is brought indoors to be tamed. The child's head is bowed, or the child's head is high, or the child's head is level, full of inherited knowledge, innate superiority. The child is taught to speak and shave and compose a sonnet and lead a people or a nation or an expedition. Sometimes the child is older, or sometimes the child is difficult, or sometimes the child is not willing to be torn from the pack, to be made to sit, stand, fetch, obey. Sometimes the child is no longer a child.

Sometimes the space between the child and the humans is wider than seasons. Sometimes the child grows up in two worlds, a beast-thing, snarling and spewing strange syntax, a deformed and hideous attempt at personhood. Sometimes the child creates a world to grow up in. This child is Atalanta, fast and strong and genderless. This child is Enkidu, friend and muse, inspiration to escape death. These children are Romulus and Remus, conquerors, builders of empires, first in a line of firsts. These children are given love tempered by fear, by worship. They are tied to the human race with a strong cord of feeling and fervor.

Sometimes there will be none of these. Sometimes there will be only a still-raw, feckless, fettered child left standing at the edge of the map, ready to push the human race into something uncharted and wild and new.

never-never

The Boys

We will never grow up. We used to tell her that all the time, our little mother in the kitchen with the frowning face and the Marcia Brady hair. Oh, boys, she would say, everyone grows up someday. Not us, we would say back. We would tell her, we will never do our own laundry, never take out the trash, never scoop the litter or get jobs or pick up after ourselves.

She is ours. She is green-grass-eyed, fire and pink through her white-icing skin. She is beautiful, our little mother, and though she is not our real mother we never remind her of that. We love her and bring her the best fruit, the brightest flowers, the most buzzing insects dumped in a jar with the lid screwed on tight.

When the jealous fairy shot her, we cleaned and dressed the wound and built her a little hut with sticks and twigs and vines, and we guarded it day and night. We guard it still. We are eating berries until we are sick, because our little mother cannot tell us to stop. We are vomiting in the under brush, we are leaving our stink outside for the crocodile to find. We are trailing the little fairy and now we are strangling her half to death until she promises us one wish and so now we are letting her go. Everyone says video games, but then our leader steps forward and says we want to be boys forever and never ever grow old.

And we all listen to our leader, so we say okay. We are saying that wish is okay with us, though we are thinking we would have liked video games, too. The littlest ones are crying but our leader puts his light hands to their faces and dries their tears and tells them to sleep. And so we sleep, and we are waiting now, waiting for our little mother to get well. Waiting forever to never grow up.

The Mother

Of course I'm not their real mother. How could I be? I'm only thirteen. I've never even kissed a boy. I've never been to a dance, except for the silly little dances they invent for themselves and their imaginary friends. I've never made out in a movie theater, never lost my virginity in the backseat of some car. Never been dumped and cried over it. Never fallen in love. I've never had a wedding, never even been proposed to. Never developed a tan line on my left hand under a thick wedding band. Never had a love of my own. Just theirs. And now my heart is stuck through and weeping, a little wooden arrow, undoing all of my love. All of it escaping through a tiny hole and still no one understands how much I want it back, how it hurts to lose it, how I will wither and die without it in this small and pathetic leaf-shack built by overgrown boys who don't quite realize how much like men they already are.

The Leader

I love her. The mother. In ways that aren't anything like appropriate. I dream about her sometimes, at night, and I wake up wet and panting like one of the dogs after a long swim. I know it's too late for me; I made that wish for the others. They can always love her for everything pure and good and true that she is, can cry and be comforted by her soft fingers. I think of those fingers, small and graceful and white, and I think of them in places they shouldn't be, places I shouldn't even know about but somehow do, and I think about how we are beautiful, proud things, she and I.

I should not be burdened with all of these feelings, leaden and acid all at once and coming up in my brain like a new kind of bile. I know it will drive us apart, these feelings, will send her so far away from me, from us. These are dangerous times, a dangerous age for us to be always on the brink of, to be rolling over like tanks over land mines. We should be sky-sailors, always. We should be dream-bringers, pain-healers, and yet now she lies in pain and may never fly with me again. I can only think of what she is to me. Of what she is to my world and how small it will shrink down without her.

The Queen of the Fairies

A door without mystery is just an open door. We are the total histories of wind, of weather, and no one could be hungrier than I for love, always love. But he is in love with her, though he foolishly wishes he weren't, and so she will vanish in the wake of events like green fields under a wall of water.

I am not of this world. I am not of any world, and I am not bothered by these feelings he speaks of. I am vengeance, I am small but mighty, I am a silver thunderbolt flung down from the gods and I show no mercy. In the age of vending machines I have survived by wrapping myself in massive shadows, in the darkness of a different time. I will not be sorry for one small girl or a pack of wild boys, not when I have seen my own children dead and gone for eons. I live and sometimes love and when I do, the world must watch its back. It is the only way to live forever.

cocoon

The children's choir has come to sing carols to the old people, just like they do every year. When the children arrive at the senior center they see the old people seated in neat rows of metal folding chairs and in beige polyester slacks.

The old people smile at them, all pink sticky gums and few teeth. A hasty conference is arranged among the children, and a quick consensus is reached: the old people smell nothing like roses. More like musty towels and mold, like stacks of newspapers and magazines buried under dust and slipcovers. And their heads move too much when they talk. It's funny and creepy, the children all agree.

When the children finish singing "O Holy Night," another old person enters the hall and heads for an empty chair in the back. The children watch him, mesmerized by his measured, glacial pace. The skin drapes off his wrists and elbows and flops about. Old people, whispers Anna to her brother, are actually half-robot. Only a robot could walk that slow. If they were people, they would fall right over.

And, says Jeff Stephens, it takes forever for old people to just, like, walk into a restaurant, and then like three hundred years to eat their food, and then like four decades to quit talking about old people stuff, like popping pills and who's dead or dying, and then it takes like sixteen centuries for them to get back in the car.

The children start the next song, the one where Chris Otelo has a solo, and the old people start to sway a little in their metal chairs. They're swaying in unison, right, left, right. The children grow uneasy; the old people have never been this active before. One of the old ladies wipes some drool from the side of her mouth. Her nails are dagger-sharp and long and pink.

The song ends and Anna's brother whispers, No one listens to the old people. At home, we just pretend to. And they try to give you things, like old batteries and pictures of people you don't even know.

Chris Otelo nods. We don't listen to our old people either, he whispers back. Ours drink half a can of Sprite, and that's it. Nothing else.

Ewww, says Anna's brother, wiping wet off his cheek. He's forgotten that Chris Otelo is a spit-whisperer.

The choir director glares at Anna's brother, and raises his hands to cue the next song. Away in a manger, no crib for a bed, the children sing. The old people stand up and push their metal chairs back, hiking elastic waistbands up under their armpits and tying terry cloth bibs around their saggy necks. The children's voices grow quieter, worried-sounding. Some children forget the words to the song. The choir director is scowling at his choir; he doesn't notice the old people shuffling forward like zombies behind him. Now they have utensils, knives in their right hands and forks in their left hands. Their hair is white and flat in the back and you can see their pink scalps underneath. They are walking like monsters with wide, deliberate steps. The children all stop, except Corey Anthony, who is nearsighted and won't wear glasses in public. The cattle are lowing, he sings, and then trails off, realizing no one else is singing.

The choir director turns around, finally, but it is too late; one of the old people stabs him in the neck with a fork and blood sprays out from somewhere near his vocal cords. The children scream and try to run, but it's like a movie: the old people are slow but many, and they surround the children, coming close enough for the choir to see the brown scabs on their faces and their tiny, murderous eyes.

The children are savory and tender, more delicious than the Grand Slam breakfast at Denny's. The old people pick bits of children from between their remaining teeth and smile big, camera-ready smiles. They are as full and friendly as babies.

Happy New Year, they say to each other.

you will be the living equation

I. Practice Problems

You should know this before the first blast turns you cold, before the first wave of sympathy strikes: there will always be two kinds of people. The first kind will want to tell you about the time their dog died, or their best friend died, or their father or wife or child or aunt or grandmother died. This is fine; this is necessary. This is how they measure grief or pain or loss, and the raw, hard cost of death.

The second kind will sit with you in silence. They will have nothing to say, because they will understand that pain is not something that can be shared or solved, that pain is not a checklist or a questionnaire. They will understand that pain is not only loss, is not only sad, is not only one thing and not sometimes another thing altogether. That pain is not quantitative, but that it can be marked off with chalk lines on a cell wall just the same. That pain is not a landscape, and yet we carefully map its roads, its quick peaks, its long dips and even the smudges on the page that obscure intention and effect. That pain is not psychic, but that it does sometimes offer a moment of brief, bright clarity.

That pain is not you, but it is yours, and you cannot return it ever. That it will be with you like an old war wound or a scarred-over burn, even when you've forgotten what it means or where it came from or who drilled it into your skin, when the very first nerve ache began.

II. Subtraction

Well, here's something awful. This is what your mind will say to you, stalwartly, like an old British colonel. *Well, here's something awful;* while you lay yourself down across the living room floor, carpet fibers carving creases into your cheek and palms. Oh, my God, your mother will say. Since childhood she has been best friends with Danny's mother, but she will not cry and you will fight about that later and often.

Holy shit, your best friend Marie will say, and she *will* cry, and for that you will accuse her of being in love with Danny ever since the three of you were small.

You were always jealous! you will shout, and fling your arm out like Sarah Bernhardt, and she will never forgive you. Years later, you will bump into one another in a department store and smile too much. You will be flustered because she has grown thin and pretty, and because when you were both eight you made all of your Barbies lesbians, though you didn't know the word then, and you swore a pact never to have anything to do with boys. You both hated Danny, because when he and your brother played *Star Wars* they made you be Princess Leia, even though you wanted to be Darth Vader and fight with a light saber. And poor, fat Marie always had to be Jabba the Hutt.

This is your first death, and it will slightly separate you from your mind. It will turn you and your mind into cordial neighbors. At first your mind will try to give counsel, will say things like: *Come on old girl, stiff upper lip* and all that. And: *Now then, mustn't carry on so.* Your mind has always been embarrassed by excess.

Your body will ignore your mind. It will learn new tricks all on its own, tricks like: curling up into a ball at the foot of the bed. And: betraying you utterly in front of absolute strangers. It will become desperate to telegraph your grief. When you think people may have forgotten about Danny, it will force you to remind them by bursting into tears during AP Psych and also sometimes by fainting in the middle of Homeroom.

This is not to say that your sadness will only be acted. Truly, you will feel small and lost and separated, just a bit, as if someone has strung a bed sheet between you and everyone else. Your teachers will sympathize and award you just-passing grades, even when the only homework you turn in all semester is a comparative study of Anne Boleyn and Danny. Over egg salad sandwiches in the lunchroom and well out of your hearing, your European History teacher will remark to your Senior Choir teacher that any common sense you used to possess must have been drained drop by drop over the last few months.

Your classmates will not be so kind. Corey Fletcher will tell everyone that you're a drama queen, milking tragedy for all it's worth. Marie will tell everyone that you're just as crazy as Danny was. *She'll probably slit her wrists eventually*, you'll overhear her telling her new friends as you pass by her locker. You will be sent home that day for putting a long deep scratch down the side of Marie's face with your painted-black-on-purpose fingernails.

Eventually you will reject all of your friends, especially the ones that didn't cry.

And especially the ones that did.

You will want desperately to talk about Danny, but no one will let you. Don't dwell on it, your mother will say. You'll make yourself ill. When you call your brother at college to ask about the afterlife, he'll tell you not to be so morbid. You'll ask him if it was morbidity or genius or both that led Mary Shelley to write *Frankenstein*.

Neither, he'll say. It was a parlor game.

You'll think about killing yourself. Of course you will. For a moment you'll picture yourself floating among water lilies and reeds, hair and skirts spread like Ophelia or the Lady of Shalott. You'll murmur, the web flew out and floated wide, but since this really isn't applicable to your situation, and since when you were ten you almost drowned in your neighbors' pool and it really was quite horrible, and since you can't think of any other poetic way to die that wouldn't hurt just as much, you decide not to.

Your body will seem strange and fragile to you. Your skin will feel like paper and your bones will feel like porcelain and you'll eat almost nothing but fruit, which you'll crave like you are pregnant. In fact, your parents will begin to worry aloud that you are pregnant, until you start pointedly leaving tampon applicators smeared with blood in their wicker wastebasket.

Your father will grow silent and sad. You are his favorite and one night he will make pancakes shaped like your initials, just like when you were little. You will refuse to eat them and he will tip them into the garbage disposal one by one, then flip the switch and stand there, listening to the loud whir and scrape of metal on metal, staring at the buttermilk bits disappearing down the drain.

III. Solve for X

Your mother—as always, as ever—will be the strong one. She will be stoic at first, then angry, and finally, exasperated. She will take you to a therapist, who will tell you to cut it out with the fruit already; don't you know you can get sick from too much vitamin C? You'll wonder how he knew; your mother must have told him. Bitch, you will think, and decide to be rebellious. You don't need a therapist. You don't need anybody.

That's your decision, of course, the therapist will say. You will roll your eyes and sigh loudly. But, he will add, it might be good for you to have someone to talk to. Your mother tells me this is your first death; you've never dealt with anything like this before. You will hear the words, First Death, with Emily Dickinson capitals, and you will panic. You will think, *Good lord, will there be more of these?* You will think of all your future loves lined up like tin soldiers in an oven, colorful and shiny, melting down as you look on in horror. And you will think you may have a Nervous Breakdown right then and there.

The therapist, whose name is Dr. Mueller, will agree to see you twice a month. In the waiting room he will tell your mother that unless you're feeling better by fall you should postpone college for a while, even though you've already been accepted. Fine by me, you'll say, and shrug.

She's lost a lot of weight, your mother will stage whisper to Dr. Mueller. You will feel like a punk. You will feel embarrassed and cool, like a rock star talking about politics.

At this point your mind will want to get away from you. It will start to take trips, to watch birds or catalogue flowers or read calm novels where no one dies in tights or duels. It will grow squeamish at the sight of your now awkward, angled body. It will avoid mirrors. You will wave whenever you spot your mind in passing, but it will duck its head and pretend not to notice. I've lost my mind, you will complain to your mother.

I know, she will say, the corners of her mouth white and sagging. She has no imagination and counts out an exact number of chocolate chips before making cookies. That's why you're seeing Dr. Mueller.

Dr. Mueller will ask you to call him Curtis and will act more like a teacher than a doctor. You won't really like him, but he will listen to you talk about Danny if you want to. And you really want to. You'll tell Dr. Mueller lots of things about Danny. You'll tell him how Danny wanted to write a book about a monster so big it could swallow the whole world but because it doesn't, people worship it and call it God. It would have been a thinly veiled novelization of his religious beliefs, you will say.

Curtis will narrow his eyes a little. Are they your beliefs as well?

Oh, no, you will tell him proudly. I'm an agnostic. He will nod and ask you where you think Danny is now. I strongly suspect, you will say, that he is nowhere at all. Then you'll worry that this sounds too clinical, as if you didn't care, but Curtis will have already moved on and so you'll cry by yourself later, wrapped in your down comforter even though it's ninety degrees outside.

Another time Curtis will ask you if you could tell that Danny was depressed. Oh, sure, you will say. Yeah, for sure. This will be a lie. You will feel that it would look bad for you of all people not to have noticed, not to have known.

IV. Undiscovered Equations

The summer will drift along in lonely clusters like tumbleweed. You'll spend it alone and bored, falling asleep at odd times. You'll go driving through thunderstorms, so slowly and aimlessly that drivers behind you will honk, giving you the finger and mouthing like fish behind their rain-spattered windows. You'll learn to read Tarot cards, training yourself to find meaning in everything. You'll find Danny in nothing: not in the romance novels from the local library, not in the Victorian poets you're reading because you think you should, not in the movies you watch, sometimes several a day, where somebody has died or is dying.

You'll start to miss your mind. While you are reading Danny's emails for the four-hundredth time, you'll want to cry but nothing will happen. You'll push air out of your lungs, force a cry, even squeeze your stomach like a squeaky toy. This will not work; it will feel more like the dry heaves than sorrow.

You'll sit for a moment and think hard. Then you'll go downstairs. I think I want to go to college this fall, you will tell your parents while they are watching television.

Your father will nod, carefully watching dancing stars instead of you. He will act as though there was a spell and his moving or speaking could break it. Your mother will annoy you by hugging you so hard that your bra clasp cuts your skin. And your mother is not the hugging type, which is no doubt why she gets it wrong.

To your surprise, you will immensely enjoy yourself at college. Your roommate will sleep too much and listen to bad house music, but she'll be funny and sarcastic. You'll gain the freshman fifteen, which is good because then you'll be rounded instead of angled. You'll take Philosophy 101 and feel sorry for Danny, because he would have loved college and now he'll never be any smarter; he'll never know any more than he did at seventeen.

One day a flyer will go up in your dorm, announcing auditions for *A Midsummer Night's Dream*. You will audition and land the part of Helena. An older girl named Tanya will play Titania because of her height and her long red hair, and the two of you will become friends. It will be good to have a friend again.

Your parents will call every day at first, then less often when they discover you're always busy. When you apologize for not visiting, your father will practically yell into the phone, No, no, stay busy, honey! That's fine, that's good!

You will sometimes forget about Danny. Then you'll feel guilty and try to cry, but it will feel like bad acting, an echo of someone else's sadness. Besides, the noises you make will annoy your roommate. You sound like a goddamn cow, she'll say.

Your parents will come to see your play and also, to your acute embarrassment, will Jeannie, Danny's mother. She will hug you and cling to you and whisper hoarsely, I wish Danny could have see you up there, he would have loved it. And you won't know what to say because Danny hated theatre. It just isn't as *specific* as film, he'd said, and you never knew what he meant so it always made you mad.

Jeannie will smell like soap and smoke. How sad, your mother will whisper to your father, she must've started smoking again, and

Jeannie will hear and turn pink and white. She will also smell a little *like* Danny, though not really like Danny but like his house. Still. There will be something unnerving about her, a reminder of Danny that you maybe don't want or need. You will resent this, and smile at her a little too coldly.

Excuse me, you will say, but I have to go backstage and change out of my costume now.

On your next visit to Curtis (you still haven't quite found your mind, though it's been coming around more often) he will tell you that perhaps this was not the kindest way you could have behaved.

Oh, you will say sarcastically, really? Sadly, it is the only retort you will be able to think of. You will be mortified. You will respond with silence for the rest of the session, finally giving Curtis two tickets to your play and driving back to the dorm in a huff to run lines with Tanya.

No one ever has any *practical* solutions for anything, you will complain.

I have one, she will say, and smile. She will tell you about a cast party that Oberon, played by a sophomore named Dan, is throwing that night. At the party, you will get drunk as a lord. You'll stumble around Oberon/Dan's house with your tongue loose and thick and a warm blanket around your brain. Oh, sorry, you'll keep saying as you bump into furniture, and everyone will laugh, mostly good-naturedly. At some point Puck will corner you in the hallway and you'll be swept away

by his sparkly eyebrows and pointy ears.

The next morning, you'll wake up on Dan/Oberon's couch, headachy and mouthcottony and feeling altogether wretched. And suddenly, before you can get up, before you can even really move, you'll start weeping. You'll know then what those Victorians poets meant when they used the word, weep: a faucet in your face, pushing out tears. You will cry the way that you never cried for Danny even when you really, really meant it. But you won't be crying for Danny. You won't know why you're crying, but it will seem that this cry might be good. It will seem that this cry might be the kind a person is supposed to have: cathartic, healing, devastating. A revelation. A hard pinch. A sharp pain to remind you you're awake.

And you will look up and there—*there* your mind will be, standing sheepishly with its hands in its pockets, scuffling its feet a little. *I got bored*, it will say.

Oh! you'll shout, queasy and swollen and relieved. Oh, it's you! I've missed you! You will sigh and try to hold still so your mind can get settled.

Shup…tryna sleep, someone will mutter from the vicinity of the floor, but you will only smile a little. You will be comforted, and you will be full of sadness, and you will never, never be solved.

the woman across the water wore the shape of love

He never could tell if her hair was white or just a flaxen blond, if her eyes were blue or brown, or if her face was pretty. He never knew how old she was or even if she was very old indeed; her movements suggested a younger woman, sure and strong and not yet stiffened by time. But he knew he was in love with her, this woman across the lake.

Every morning she emerged from her cottage and walked the length of the pier. Or rather, she glided, her bare feet just touching the wooden slats, her dressing gown fluttering behind her like grey wings, her slim limbs light and full of the natural grace of morning.

She stood at the water's edge for hours, and sometimes, he swore she stood there for days. Sometimes she seemed to slip into the lake like fog, and sink with the swell of the moon. Sometimes he thought he heard a thin high sound, halfway between song and wail, pour out of her throat on the coldest and darkest nights.

He wondered if she was a ghost, a hallucination, a fairy who'd come through a split in the spell between worlds. Or another Circe, trying to ensnare him even across this expanse of water. His cabin was small and his days, smaller. It would not be hard, he sometimes thought, to ensnare me. I think I would become a boar for her. I think I would bear anything to see her close and real and rare.

In his best moments he thought he might have written her, so well that she flew from the page and into existence. Since he had given her nothing to do, she was able to do nothing, and sometimes he regretted that on her behalf. He wondered if he'd been careless with description, let it get away from him. Better to proceed with action. Better to let his future characters live rather than be.

He envied other men, living in cities and in love with women they could touch. He envied people who lived in brick buildings surrounded by paved streets and other brick buildings. He envied animals their ability to root in the earth around them. He seemed only able to stare and stare at the pines, the black rock, the wild lake, and her. Pale hair glowing against her drab gown. Straight and slim as a queen. The water stirring at her feet, birds circling above, the trees breeze-bent and kneeling before her. Could he steal her cloak, hide it like a skin? Could she be trapped by her own enchantment? Was she a white witch, sending water magic across his lake; was she weaving tangled messages on the waves that he couldn't undo?

The man knew that other men had died for love. He read about them in books. He wondered if he might die, too, of this tight white burn in his heart for her. He rather hoped so, after he'd awoken from a dream of swimming to her dock, emerging from the water like his own spirit, of waiting on the dock for her to swallow him whole. He wondered if her eyes were kind. He wondered if she would dissolve like pale ink in a pool if he swam too close. So he never swam close, never approached her cabin, never knew her age or her face or her name or even if she was really there at all—or if he loved but a trick of water and light, a flash of morning sun staining his cornea in the shape of a slim and lovely thing, like a woman.

vesuvius

As she watched her husband give his stump speech on TV, the senator's wife set fire to the furniture. It was a slow process, despite the gasoline, despite the extra lighter fluid she'd purchased. She had to light the curtains in five different spots. Had they purchased flame-retardant curtains? She couldn't think why she would have done such a thing; perhaps his mother had bought them. That was entirely possible; the mother-in-law liked buying things to keep the wife married to the house, things like curtains and crock pots and linens. Things like alarm systems which were not, the wife had discovered, particularly difficult to disable.

The fire trucks showed up just in time for her to catch the last of his speech. The flames were shouting obscenities by then, devouring his slick, weak words. She could see he was in a park somewhere. She could feel her lungs packing it in.

She stumbled to the front door, singed her hand on the knob, wondered whether to make her way to the kitchen and grab a potholder, but decided against it. Decided to let them find her crisped rather than crumpled and sorry on the driveway. She coughed, crouched down in front of the television to find a little more air. Her anger was her home; let it burn hot and clean through the drywall, through the insulation, through the grass and trees and houses and all of the human debris scattered like dead leaves over the surface of the world. Let anger fry the face of god.

as they always are

The mother was the mother in a time before drugs could save you from the small things. It was the small things that always got them, in the time before, and the mother's death was no different. She cut her hand on a nail, or maybe a piece of glass, or maybe the edge of the bread knife; it doesn't really matter. The end result was septicemia, which sounds pretty as a woman's name but means poison in the blood. The end result was fever, was the loss of a hand, was organ failure. The end result was death.

The mother was called the mother for a reason; the mother had a baby not long before she hurt her hand. The baby was still very new and very pink. He had greedy eyes and hungry teeth, hard and sharp as diamonds. The baby's teeth would latch into the mother's breast like tiny hooks as he fed, and when at last he ripped them free her nipples would weep blood along with milk. A dark red ring soon marked all of her blouses. The mother didn't mind, though. The mother was kind and beautiful, as the mother always is. Her hair was the color of lemons and her eyes were the color of polished steel, and the kindness in her glowed so fiercely and brightly that she could barely feel the baby's bite. Her love for the baby blocked all of the pain and the hurt and the sadness in the world.

So when the mother died, the father could find no one to feed the baby. He hired wet nurses, but the baby wouldn't take their milk, and they wouldn't take the baby's teeth. An unsentimental man, as the father always is, he married the upstairs maid—a very young woman who slept in his bed even before the mother died. The maid had no better luck than the wet nurses. Angry at her failure, she told the father his son was a demon and that she would have nothing to do it. The father tried to feed him from a bottle, tried cow's milk and goat's milk and sheep's milk, but to no avail. The baby just would not eat.

Yet, though the baby did not eat, he did not starve. His cheeks grew pinker and fatter, his head grew bigger, his greedy eyes grew brighter. He laughed and clapped his fat hands and cooed in his cradle.

You see, said the father's new wife, he is a demon child. How can he still grow and clap his hands when he has taken no milk for months? How can he laugh when he should have starved to death weeks ago?

I am troubled, the father admitted. I do not know how to answer these questions, and I am greatly troubled.

The father's new wife crossed her arms over her lovely white chest, which hid a heart grown narrow and choked with hate. Her hair was black as a moonless night, and her eyes were cold coals. It's a demon child, she repeated.

She was proud and beautiful, yes, but as false and cold as the mother had been warm and true. She was the mother's inverse, the far-flung other. The stepmother. And being what the stepmother always is, she decided to sneak and creep about at night, to spy and sit in shadows and find out who or what was feeding the baby. She meant to rid herself of the first wife's baby by proving him unholy, unnatural.

The stepmother was thin and small, and so easily hid herself behind the baby's bassinet to keep watch one night. She watched and she waited, until the moon was high and the baby began to whimper, and the curtains blew soft kisses to the rocking chair and the changing table. The warm breeze chilled her heart. She pulled her cloak tighter and then froze as something entered the room through the window; she sighed and relaxed when she saw it was only a small black cat. But no ordinary cat, she realized at once. The cat leapt to the top of the bassinet and whispered to the baby, its voice a string of whistling sibilants. Hush, child, it said. She is coming soon.

Then the child hushed, and the black cat hopped onto the windowsill and vanished out the window.

The stepmother hid her face in her hair, shivering now despite the warmth. She told herself that she had been sleeping, that she had dreamed the black cat; she pinched her thin skin and knew she was not sleeping. Scared, she started to rise and was stopped by the baby's cry and then a scraping sound at the window—another cat, one that leapt onto the baby's bassinet just like the first. This cat was white as snow, and its voice was a quiet, purring hum. Hush, my little one, it said. She is coming sooner.

Then the little one hushed, and the white cat hopped onto the windowsill and vanished out the window.

The stepmother shivered harder than ever now, and knew that she had not slept or dreamed. She was afraid, but not cowardly, and so she stayed to hear the baby cry once more. Instantly a third cat, a spotted tabby this time, leapt onto the bassinet and spoke in a voice like rustling leaves. Hush, sweet baby, it said. She is here.

And with a rush of warm wind, the dead mother appeared. She was white and translucent as rice paper and still clad in her funeral gown. But her kindness glowed more fiercely in death than in life, and the tabby cat rubbed its head against her ghostly ankles as she gently picked up the baby and sat in the rocking chair. The chair did not move, did not creak as the dead mother rocked back and forth with her baby at her breast. The sad sight would have moved almost anyone to pity, but the stepmother felt only anger burning in her throat as she watched the baby drowsily feed. She cried out, stood but could not speak through her rage, and the dead mother turned in surprise. The stepmother could see the blurred outlines of the curtains blowing right through the dead woman. The mother sighed, placed the baby back in his bassinet, and kissed him once, very softly, on his tiny forehead. Then she stared at the stepmother for a very long time before speaking.

No mortal should have seen me, she finally said in a voice like the faintest far-off stars. You've killed him now, you know. But, she said, and pointed at the stepmother, I'll make sure you're worse than dead by morning. Then without another word, she vanished out the window with the warm breeze. The tabby cat stayed behind. It tilted its head and looked up at the stepmother, its tail swishing back and forth. Then, in a quick flicker of movement, it pounced.

When the sun rose, the baby's nursemaid came to check on him as she did every morning. She found him lying on his back, eyes open and quite dead. All the fatness and pinkness had gone from him; he looked as though he'd starved to death. The window was open and the room was quite cool—and yet a strange, warm breeze seemed to linger there, caressing the cheek of the weeping nursemaid.

The stepmother, it was discovered, had disappeared and could not be found. However, a strange stain, black as a moonless night and cold to the touch, was discovered on the nursery floor behind the bassinet that day. Nothing could ever lift that spot from the floorboards, no matter how the maids might scrub and scrape. It seemed determined to stick to the floor forever. It was hardly important, though, as the stain was quite small and a rug was quickly found to keep it out of sight.

when your carcass hits the canvas

In this corner: It's the Fat Asshole! But he's moving fast, stomach spilling over the jerking, kicking body as he lunges forward, tries to pry open the foamy jaws.

And in this corner: It's the Hunted Man! The scrawny disappearing act with a white pill in his back pocket and his face all covered in glare. But underneath the nerves: his body one tight nerve strung too tight, strung to snap. He's hard to corner. Hard to pin down.

In-fighter versus out-fighter. Speed and strategy versus power, versus chin. It's a goddamned fight we've got here, folks. Until someone goes down for good. Until someone smiles real bloody for the cameras.

Program Notes

The Hunted Man: Doesn't matter that it's been ages. That he's grown old, benign. His back went years ago and he hasn't been able to lift a thing since. He's bald. Grows breathless when he walks more than a couple of blocks. Sometimes it hurts just to piss, that's what he is now. A guy who winces when he takes a piss. But they hang men like him no matter how much time has passed. Whether his remains are twitching at the end of a rope or spattered across the side of the road, doesn't much matter.

The Fat Asshole and Co.: The new muscle isn't the same as the old, back when they'd take just about anybody if they were the right kind of cruel. The new muscle is trained, professional, even if they don't look it. These guys could break your neck with two fingers. And whether they liked it or not, you'd never know.

Round One

He realizes as soon as the tall young man in the navy suit taps him on the shoulder. Even before, really: he's felt it, something breached, something broken, a current switched off. He doesn't ask. He just offers his wrists.

Let's go, says the man in the navy suit. He's not chatty. But not brutish and hard like some. This one is polite, quiet, businesslike. Doing his job.

The man in the navy suit firmly parades him down the street, and together they pretend not to notice the blinds sliding shut as they pass each rotting row house. His neighbors, registering their collective disapproval. Tomorrow, they'll have forgotten his name, too; they'll let it fly right off the tips of their tongues in their sleep, unable to summon it back if anyone bothers to make an inquiry. Not that anyone will. It wasn't his real name, anyway.

He and the man in the navy suit finally stop in front of a plain white van idling at the curb. The suit's twin is at the wheel, wearing a fatter man. Obviously the brutal type, though right now his aggression is aimed at a handful of corn chips. More talkative, too. Christ, what took so long, he asks, mouth full of chip fragments. Some fall out onto his chin, sticking to the sweat, and he wipes the mess off impatiently with a meaty fist. God, he says, it's so fucking hot out here. We gotta get them to fix this air one of these days. You know? It's like a hundred degrees in this fucking thing.

The original suit makes a sour face. Just open up the back, he says. Let's get him in.

Round Two

No window in the back. But the hunted man knows this scene. He's been through it. Once the van starts up, he tries to figure out turn by turn where they're headed. He thinks they might be driving to the old southwest station, the one that was abandoned until they rebuilt that part of town. They put up a new baseball stadium, and the stores sprang up around it like a beige rash. Ugly false-fronts, intended to provoke nostalgia for some flag or other. Some government or other. The development is called Main Street. He despises it, spits on the fake cobblestone every time he walks that way.

He wonders if he might be able to escape. Guesses not. Maybe when he was a younger man— of course, if he doesn't escape they'll kill him anyway.

Still, he thinks, shifting around on the hard plastic seat. Still, he'd like to be the one to end it, to maintain control to the last. It would be a small triumph. And there's absolutely no chance of that if he goes down trying to escape.

If he can just get hold of it—he thinks maybe, yes. Yes. One of his hands is slightly more mobile than the other, the fingers a little less crammed together. Good. He bends his elbows as much as he can before the metal starts cutting into his wrists. Damn. Not quite there. His middle finger can just touch the tip of his jeans pocket, but the handcuffs won't let him move his arms down any more. Sharp pain arcs his wrist, a knife of pain slicing up his resolve. Goddamn goddamn goddamn.

Round Three

The tires ka-thunk ka-thunk over the road. The hunted man takes a deep breath. Okay. He can be creative, even if he can't be strong or young or agile. His mind is still fit enough. Think, think. Think! After all, if they're really heading for the southwest station, they've almost arrived. He's got maybe five minutes, tops.

After some painful maneuvering, he manages to get down belly first on the floor. Facedown so close he could lick the dust and dirt and filth right off from between those white grooves. He thinks of the shoes that must have worn down those grooves, the feet filling them cramped up with misery and awful hope. Wonders about the red-brown-yellow stains spilling across the middle of the floor. Are these small remainders biology or tragedy? Just a person's sloughings, tiny pieces of hair and teeth and fingernails; what was once living is broken down to component parts. A skin flake is just a skin flake. An eyelash is just an eyelash. The body's leftovers are myriad and mean.

He works himself into a U-shape, bends his back while curling his legs upward, falls over onto his face and flails about like a retarded seal. But finally, finally, he manages to jam two fingers into his right back pocket. He feels the edges of the pill, shoves it out with his fingers. It clatters and rolls on the floor behind him as the van turns, slows, stops. A door slams, then another. Footsteps around the side. Shit. Desperately he spins around on his stomach, crawls on his knees to the corner of the van, bends his head down and spoons up the little white tablet with his curled tongue. The van doors open and the fat asshole is reaching but he's out of reach, ha ha out of reach you fuckers out of reach.

Knockout

He tastes blood, sweat, fear—all the human ruin built up in a coating on this impersonal, industrial rubber floor. He swallows down the present, then eats up the past. He puts out his own lights. The medics swing the end of the stretcher around, aim it at the open mouth of the ambulance. As they shove the stretcher in, an arm slips out from under the sheet, fist up, purple circles inked around the dead white wrist. Just lines on skin, just lines on skin on bones. Soon to separate and fall away for good.

be like us and we will like you maybe

The mother sits on the side of the couch that the mother always sits on. The long weight of her has bent the couch cushion into a shallow V shape. Sofa, she thinks. Her daughter is forever telling her not to say 'couch,' that only rural people say 'couch' and 'crick.' Her daughter cares very deeply about these things.

The mother is impatient. She half-watches her daughter taking down a message and half-watches Anderson Cooper saving babies on the television. She clears her throat. Twice.

The daughter pauses, phone in hand; she pretends to be sardonic. Well, she says. He hasn't been eaten by sharks or sucked out of an airplane window or shot with a spear gun. Which is what we all expected, yes?

The mother sighs. So, what then?

The daughter reads from her notes. He drowned, Mother. Heart attack in the pool. He was not alone, of course. She rolls her eyes, says into the phone, yes, thank you. We'll be in touch. Yes, yes, you too. Goodbye.

The young one? The Mexican woman?

Cuban, Mother. She's Cuban. The daughter frowns at her expensive wristwatch. I have to get going, she says. Will you be okay?

No, says the mother. Did you tell your sister?

Ha, laughs the daughter without laughing. Ha, ha, ha. Her sister has been missing in mind forever, missing in body for years. No one can find her, but their mother seems to think the daughter has a telephone in her head, a direct line to the sister that lives on the moon.

Go, says the mother. Anderson Cooper is smiling at the viewers, and he's holding up a small child like a bowling trophy. She's safe now, he says. He is so reassuring.

After her daughter has left the mother picks up the pad, reads her daughter's neat, angry notes scattered like shouts across the page. DAD, thunders the notepad. HEART IN SWIM POOL! AND GOOD!! WHAT ABOUT HOUSE? FIND OUT!!! The last sentence—the extreme imperative—underlined three times.

I don't want the house, the mother tells Anderson Cooper.

I know, he says, I know. You never want anything, do you? He approaches the couch, begins removing the rubble that surrounds the mother, as if she were a small child to be salvaged. Remain seated, he says courteously. Be saved.

•

The sister doesn't live on the moon. But she might as well. She lives on the 41st floor of an enormous building, in a tiny apartment surrounded by quiet carpets and nice older couples. They bake her cookies and brownies and bread and tell her to eat, eat. She eats but can't swallow, speaks but can't spit out the words. They clog like the food in her throat and it always reminds her of how she tried but couldn't wedge her fingers between the nylon and her neck, the way they always do on TV. It was dark and she couldn't see, but she managed, just before the sirens sounded, to put a long deep scratch down the side of his face.

Here on the 41st floor, men sometimes shimmer into being, like dreams skating soundlessly through the apartment. She meets them all with calm posture, violent headaches. She knows she is supposed to be enjoying her youth and her body and men in her youthful body. But every man that appears, her eyes linger on his cheeks. She brings only beardless men to bed.

Late at night when they are sleeping, she licks her finger and scrubs hard at their skin, just to be sure. Just to be certain of the smooth terrain.

•

The daughter finds it is getting harder to say no. The world keeps asking, and she is, if not kind, at least polite. She has been brought up to believe refusal as rude as spitting. So she caves at last and says, fine. Fine. I'll make a baby. Because the approval of the world is important to her. The world's approval tastes like chocolate cake with butter cream frosting, which is, after all, her favorite.

So she heads down to the basement, drags out the dinged-up toolbox, sets up the sawhorses and puts plastic over the floor. She straps on her safety goggles and makes sure the cats are locked out, so they won't get curious about the circular saw. Then she switches on the power and picks up her tools, and she builds a baby.

She builds him out of pine, with a toggle up the middle so he'll stand up straight. She hammers blocks into the corners of the boards to hold him together. Then she nails unbleached muslin to his frame, and uses waterproof paints to give him her black hair, her brown eyes, her small stubby hands and her mauve-and-white skin. She paints some baby clothes on him for decency: blue coveralls with yellow ducks lined up across the front, and a navy t-shirt matched with navy socks and navy plaid boaters. She sets him up in the front window, so the world can see him and know he is perfect and hers.

But the cats don't like him. They keep nosing at him and scratching his back with their claws, until his supports finally go and he falls to the floor in a flat cloud of sawdust. The cats take turns peeing on the baby's mauve-and-white face until it is mauve-and-white-and-goldenrod instead.

The daughter watches, disgusted. The baby doesn't cry or laugh or move. What kind of baby is this? The daughter looks out the window and sees the world pointing, calling names, laughing at a woman who couldn't make a baby that would last. The daughter wonders what it would be like to love a thing you made, a thing that was you in so many ways and yet not you in all the ways that matter most. She wonders what it would be like, to live with love. To live with even just the hope of something like it.

the wives are turning into animals

The husbands are almost sure of it. They have strong memories of an earlier time, of the wives with soft smooth faces and ten fingers and toes.

But lately, things have changed. Some of the wives have grown scaly patches, or sprouted thick pelts. Some of the wives have shrunk considerably. White, wide wings have unfolded, horns have appeared, tongues have grown longer and rougher and pinker, noses wetter and more sensitive than before.

The husbands have grown uneasy at night, listening to the wheezing and snorting of the wives as they sleep, as they embrace their husbands with tentacles and talons and long tails. The husbands aren't sure what to do, whether to say something. They wonder if it would be rude to ask about the wives' new appetites, their sudden hunger for mice and mealworms and raw, wriggling fish. They worry that they won't be able to keep their ravenous wives fed. They worry that the neighbors will complain about the carcasses littering their lawns.

The husbands worry, most of all, that their wives will finally fly or crawl or swim away, untethered from the promises that only humans make or keep.

the only story in the world

Father

He is too fond of the child, for all the wrong reasons. He hangs success higher and higher, a star out of reach, hoping this will expand the child's capacity for wishing. But the child never looks up at the night sky. Sirius lopes along unseen, Canopus steers his ship in vain. The child is firmly rooted to the earth. Her eyes are a steady lantern; they light the way over the rough and raw terrain.

Mother

She washes the child every night, a scrawny thing white and smooth as the tub she stands in. The child shivers and goose pimples pop up all over her paper skin, over dark purple veins, mauve pools under the young/old eyes. The mother understands that her child is special; as she towels off the drops of wet she tells the child, You are a thin strong weed, born to rule. You were born to take care of us. You were born to take care of us all.

Child

The child is wiser than her parents, as all children are. The child understands the world is made of disappointment. Nothing the child wants has ever come to pass since the earliest days; once the child's desires grew more complex the world began to say no, and has kept on saying no ever since.

People say spoiled and the child does not understand, the child can never understand. People say spoiled and what they really mean is the innocence of children, and what they really mean is something that does not exist, has never existed, will never exist as long as there are years to stretch a life into and no way to stop the stretching.

Home

A house, a hut, a village, a mound, a grove, a flat, an apartment, an alley, a meadhall, a basement, a condo, a truck, a car, a trailer, a dirt floor, a castle, a thatched cottage, a church, a sanctuary, a stronghold, a storefront, a hospital, a park bench, a bed, a grave.

Growth

Love, fear, and habit. Three things that will grow in you and hold you fast, no matter the chemical makeup of your soul. They will be stubborn tumors in the dank dark of your insides. No matter how your beleaguered blood tries to expel them.

Heart

A fist in your face; a red, rotten face in your chest. It tells things. It told the mother she would be better loved elsewhere, told the father he'd never really loved her at all. It told the child she would bask in the warmth of the cities we build, but also that she would burn in their ruins. This was the saddest part of the story, this discovery.

The heart said, Child, you will wander the world and bring happiness to all you meet, and the world will make you its favorite daughter. But even you must come to an end. And this is the terrible prophecy that we hold close and secret. This is the always-whisper in our ear.

Land

The soil is blowing away like loose words; the earth sheds our short history here like skin flakes after a bath. The earth is cleansing itself of us. There is a hungry safety in our movements, like we're scared to move too fast. We might blur ourselves; we might be here then gone, which we suppose will happen someday, but why hurry things along?

The meat of movement fills us beyond question, beyond dream, and our heels dig in the dust in vain. The whole world is a chair of gold and our lives are etched into its seat, like pictures of the future for our ancestors to discover.

War

The guns have been sitting in storage for a very long time. We alone know the location, the combination to enter. We alone know where the ammunition is kept. We alone know how to use these massive weapons, how to roll the girdles over the spiked tires to keep them from sinking into the mud, how many horses it takes to pull them out of the shed and into the field, how to tell which shells will fire what: incendiary charges, high explosive charges, or gas. We alone know the bodies strewn on the grass, casualties of mass action and opposing forces.

We keep these things a secret from the child, because we know how eager she is. But lately, she has been driving us mad with questions, circling while we plow our fields, while we watch television. She keeps asking about the guns, about the last war, about the war before that. She keeps asking us about the body and the soul, and the way the two can fuse together and fall apart.

Is that a war? she asks. We tell her, no, that is a weapon.

She looks to us, this child who is no longer a child. She has forgotten to be a savior, to keep pushing forward. She burns to divide and to kill. She burns to blow another's cells apart with differences. It's time, she says. Tell me how, she says. Tell me how to fight the war.

Fire

So she was burnt, with all her clothes,

> And arms, and hands, and eyes, and nose;
> Till she had nothing more to lose
> Except her little scarlet shoes;
> And nothing else but these was found
> Among her ashes on the ground.*

Sleep

What existed before home. The Ur-Home. The thing we all come back to in the end. Home to all, monsters and mermaids and children and parents, mortals and immortals, questions and dreams. The bright hall for heroes and the long dark depths for the rest of us.

The thing we build with our useless, heavy hands and hope will enfold us when we are going. When we are gone.

Darkness

As in: afraid of the. As in: a candle in the. As in: the endless sleep of.

---

*Excerpt from "The Dreaded Story of the Matches," in Der Struwwelpeter, by Heinrich Hoffman

most of them would follow wandering fires

XI. The return is the most difficult part; the thin membrane that separates the world from the quest is harder than diamond. The hero pushes, he leans, he tries to reorder his atoms in the shape of a shepherd, a monk, a maiden. He slips through the world barrier sideways, but his sword catches on the air and shatters the calm into pieces. The townspeople whisper and bring him t-shirts and photos to sign; the hero smokes a cigarette and tries to look casual. His heart is already aching for the high grasslands, the mysterious marshes, the dark forests with demons to catch and trails to follow. His heart is already beating faster in the slowness of the world.

X. The wound in his side smells rotten, stinks like death. He lies on his back like Prometheus, chained by pain and exhaustion. He watches the hawks circle overhead and thinks of his love, of the gold in her voice and hair, her hot pink toenails pushing into his calf while he tries to shake her awake from her nightmare. Her breasts soft round peaches in satchels. He groans and tries to rise, but stars rush to his eyes and he falls back. Dirt mixes with blood and pus. Hot winds blow through him, and he gropes for his cell phone. He needs a rescue. It is the truth, in the end: all heroes need rescuing after the quest is through. All heroes fall into themselves like empty clothes when the aim stops burning, when the last light has left the lining of their throats and they begin to be ordinary again.

IX. They ride out of hell with their prize held high. Swords out, car windows down, they sweep inevitable as locusts through wild, through wind, through wet and ocean that would swallow a dead man. They fly faster than angels, as just is their cause. But they are followed by the stink of fear and the smell of death, and hurt spills from fresh wounds because they are only human, strange and soft a thing as that can be. Shields hard, they flee because they cannot fight. Swords high, they flee because they will die, but not yet. Not today.

VIII. And there, in the clearing filled with light, the ultimate boon. It glitters flat, scratched and faded, this odd plain object of their quest. So much blood has soaked the ground in the seeking for it. The gods have starved in hunger for it. Heroes have shed their lives for it; villains have paid whole souls for it, and all the while, no one wondering what will become of the world when it is found. No one wondering where the rain will fall, if all the tables are heavy with plenty and the soldiers as gentle as lambs.

VII. At the top of the tower, a mirror. A face glowering back in the dim light, heavy-browed and dark with shame. A prophecy of doom, of twin destroying twin, son murdering father. The fields are on fire outside. The burning crops smell like late fall back in the town, like the homecoming bonfires, like the children's stray voices, begging a penny for the Guy. Like closed eyes and deep breaths. Like the womb.

VI. Things that will tempt you to stray from the path: a woman, a battle, a bag of gold, a sword, a gun, a stack of jeans, a crown, a letter, a baseball, a pipe, a half-pipe, a fortune-teller's tell, a green monster, a monstrous ambition, a starring role, a huge breakfast, a bottle of wine, a bed and a fire and a very good book. The hammock your dad strung between the two big oak trees; the space that he made for you where his knees drew in, when you were so small you could press your whole face into one rope square and watch the ground swaying, swinging up to meet you again and again.

V. It doesn't really matter who she is, whether wife, mother, sister, aunt, grandmother, stepmother, goddess, saint, fairy, queen, or angel. The point of her appearance is to give them respite, to vary the pace and to provide a dream for reference. Later, when they are tired as earth—when they are hungry as fire, when thoughts are murky and dark as the great ocean depths—the dream will give them succor. Later, the dream will give them strength. Back on their feet, sword in hand, they will worship but not understand the lady. They won't understand that she is stronger than warriors, for her strength is endless and boundless. They won't understand that she needs no weapons, only the vast reservoir of dream to draw upon, to bottle up and distribute to wandering heroes. They will brush this great gift from their boots like dust at the end of the day, and she will not mind. She is made for this fate, after all. She is the world's loveliest vending machine.

IV. Head out the door and stop for a moment; notice the copse of trees to your left and the town on your right. Remember how far you've never been before, notice the dead trees among the living and hope this is not a bad omen. Shudder slightly. Turn right. Find the dark magician in his foreclosed exurban home, and do battle. If you survive, leave the house and take the second left. Drive twenty miles to the nearest gas station and while you are filling up, find a tearful old lady who begs you to catch the thief who stole her purse. Explain that you are not the police, and that you are on a quest, but feel so sorry for the old woman, who reminds you of your grandmother back home, that you give chase anyway. Catch the thief, who turns out to be a servant of the dark magician. Find out from him where his boss's lair is now located. Turn left. Drive ten miles through darkening, dense air and roll up your windows when the smog starts to push in. Continue to drive, seeking the lair but lost, mapless, blind, unsure of what to do or where to go and positive you've made all the wrong choices. Blame the old lady, blame the thief, blame your father for not stopping you, and your girlfriend for urging you on. Cry like a girl. Be glad no one can see you, but of course this is a quest and so everything is public. Everyone is watching. Everyone is waiting for you to get on with it. Get on with it.

III. Wizards use many weapons with varying degrees of proficiency, but do not use armor or shields. A wizard casts spells, which must be chosen and prepared ahead of time. A wizard need not be strong, but a wizard must possess intelligence, and rest well before casting spells. A wizard may purchase a familiar, to assist him with magical tasks and provide companionship. A wizard may also present magical boons and tokens to help the hero on his journey, if the wizard so chooses. The wizard may not interfere with the hero's quest in any other way, though out of love and loyalty the wizard may choose to say the hell with it, and join the hero in saving the world or doing his best to try.

II. It starts with a stranger, or a close friend, but never a casual acquaintance. There must be something impassioned about the relationship, a love or a danger or both. There must be something to prove to this messenger, this strange herald who is unable to take up the task and must pass it on to another. Fate must choose, or judgment must choose, or love must choose, or all three in conjunction with the right or wrong planets. The new hero must be very lucky, or very unlucky, or perhaps he does not believe in luck at all. Perhaps he has already decided, long ago, that if such an offer were made he would grab at the chance. Perhaps he has sought such an offer. Perhaps he has fastened his hopes tight to this day, has kept watch for the moment when his best friend's eyes, or a stranger's eyes, or his father's or uncle's or brother's eyes move heavenward, just slightly, before coming to rest on the hero's ready shoulders at last.

I. The hero who is not yet the hero sits on a hill near a pasture, thinking of brighter things than cows and corn. He fills his dreams with sports cars, with travel, with books that look different than the books here, and women who look different from the women here. He flicks his lighter, tips his cigarette with fire. He sighs to see his father approaching. The day will be ordinary, he supposes, like every day. The day will be chores, one big chore to forget and resume tomorrow.

The hero who is not yet the hero watches his father and worries he is starting to resemble him. He worries his life will be tedium, corn and cows, bills, endless mouths to feed, worry lines etched deep into a sun-spotted brow. But he doesn't worry too much; he changes the channel in his head and thinks of his girlfriend's hair, bright gold in the sun and sparkling like champagne. Of her eyes, blue and round as marbles. Of her breasts, downy and small. He thinks he could stick around for breasts like those.

He smiles and takes a last drag, grinds the cigarette butt into the soft dirt, watches the sun creep up into the sky, little by little. He thinks, yes, it would be worth it, to stick around here for his girl, for his father, for sunrises like these. For the beginnings of days to cycle back around and renew themselves, warm as embers, familiar already as home on the day he came into this world.

acknowledgements

This book owes its existence to many human bodies. Please keep in mind that since I am an imperfect human body, I will almost certainly leave people off this imperfect list. If I've left you off, please know that I am almost certainly still overflowing with gratitude toward you.

Thank you first and foremost to the editors and staff at the following publications where these stories first appeared: *Unsaid, elimae, Bust Down the Door and Eat all the Chickens, New Dead Families, Annalemma, Necessary Fiction, trnsfr, Bluestem, matchbook, Buffalo's Art Voice, A Capella Zoo, Splinter Generation, Wigleaf, Corium, Everyday Genius, Tiny Hardcore Press, decomP, Storyglossia, Smokelong Quarterly, The Collagist, Titular, Gargoyle and Paycock Press, Dark Sky,* and *Barrelhouse.* (David, Brandon, Bradley, Zack, Christopher, Steve, Alban, Roxane, Edward, Greg, Colin, Alan, Scott, Lauren, Adam and Alec, Jason, Anne and Steven, Tara, Matt, Reynard, Richard, Brian and Kevin and Christy and Gabe, and Dave, I hold you responsible for this book starting to be a thing.)

Thank you to Greg Gerke, Michael Kimball, Jen Michalski, Kirsty Logan, Michelle Reale, Paula Bomer, Christopher Newgent, Scott Garson, JA Tyler, Molly Gaudry, Mark Cugini, Amelia Gray, Ben Loory, Jason Jordan, xTx, Sal Pane, Mel Bosworth, John Madera, Tom Williams, and all the writers and editors and readers and blurbers and reading series organizers and all-round terrific human beings who made me feel welcome right away in what for me has been a brave new world.

Thank you to Dave Housley and Roxane Gay for more or less introducing me to that world and helping me find my footing there so many times.

Thank you to my wonderful editors and all the staff at Curbside Splendor. You've made this the best, most positive experience I could imagine and I couldn't ask for a more supportive or hard-working team.

Thank you to Alban Fischer for making my book gorgeous and perfect and exactly what I'd somehow wanted it to be without knowing what that was.

Thank you to Robert Kloss, Matt Bell, Lauren Becker, Steve Himmer, and Erin Fitzgerald for being such fine readers and editors and writers and teachers and collaborators and cheerleaders and mentors and truth-tellers and most of all, friends. I owe you guys more beers than we will ever have time to drink.

Thank you to Loki, Neela, Vesta, and Ilsa, the non-humans who hung out in all the highest places of my life while I was writing this book.

Thank you and so much love to my mom and dad, who wish that I wrote happier stories, but who have always been unendingly supportive and proud of my melancholy madness just the same.

And thank you most of all to Chris, who's had to put up with me for nine years now and has somehow managed to be nothing but encouraging and steadfast and awesome. He is, and always has been, my better half.

AMBER SPARKS's fiction has been widely published in
journals and anthologies, including *New York Tyrant, Unsaid, Gargoyle,
Barrelhouse,* and *The Collagist.* This is her first full-length short story
collection. She lives in Washington, D.C. Find her at
www.ambernoellesparks.com and on Twitter @ambernoelle.

CURBSIDE SPLENDOR

WWW.CURBSIDESPLENDOR.COM

The Waiting Tide
poems by Ryan W. Bradley,
a bilingual homage to Pablo Neruda's *The Captain's Verses*
(Concepcion Books, Spring 2013)

The Typewriter Stories
by Franki Elliot
(Summer 2013)

Life Stories
by Chicago writer Samantha Irby
(Fall 2013)

JOURNALS

Curbside Splendor
a bi-annual journal that celebrates urbanism

Another Chicago Magazine
a bi-annual themed journal
(www.antoherchicagomagazine.net)

AND MORE TO COME...

CPSIA information can be obtained at www.ICGtesting.com
Printed in the USA
LVOW121509181012

303458LV00009B/10/P